The Winding Road

Rosalie T. Turner

and The Tuesday Breakfast Group

ISBN: 1508465703
ISBN 13: 9781508465706

Members Of The Tuesday Breakfast Group

Alma Bock
Evelyn Bochow
Valerie Byrd
Dean Calhoun
Lynn Coulam
Jackie Covey
Earlene Durand
Margie Evans
Sharron Harris
Sylvia Hornback
Becky Jones
Sarah Kangerga
Marcie Klinger
Melanie Mantooth
Jan Mika
Linda Nelson
Pat Pangrac
Karen Pettersen
Vernett Safford
Carolin Sanders
Susan Stuart
J.Sue Topping
Bobbie Turk
Rosalie Turner
Sherry Vacik
Doris Weaver

Prologue

Darkness to light, nighttime to dawning, always the same, over and over. With the morning a new day unwinds itself like a road full of twists and turns, the moments full of the unknown. The possibilities are endless: joy and sorrow, love and hate, resentments and forgiveness, work and play, birth and, of course, . . . death.

The late June sun spilled warmth into the open jeep as it headed out of Taos. Turning at the Visitor's Center onto Route 64, it quickly pulled through the KFC drive-thru.

The driver lowered the radio's volume and ordered, "Two large cokes, please."

While they waited, the woman pulled on a baseball cap, securing the strap under her blonde ponytail. Moments later, they were on their way again. The road wound its way through the canyon, past the campgrounds full of summer visitors. The sky was cerulean blue, intense in its cloudlessness.

"This is the kind of day that makes me glad to be alive, to be in this place, you know?" the woman said.

"I hope it's also because we're together," replied the man.

A pause, then she answered, "Of course."

They rode in silence for a while, past Shady Brook, winding their way higher as they both savored the vista around them.

"Have you thought any more about what I asked you earlier?" said the man.

"You mean about next weekend?"

"Uhhuh. It'll be a nice getaway. We'll have a good time."

The woman sighed, "I don't think I'm ready for that. It's . . . it's complicated."

"I don't see what's so complicated. If you prefer, we can each have our own room when we get there. It's only about having companionship on a trip to Denver, that's all; someone to have dinner with after the meeting I have to attend. We could go to a movie or something."

"I'll think about it," she said.

They slowed around the hairpin curve for the last climb up the mountain, then enjoyed the sway of the open jeep as it hugged the curves. Cresting the top, the vehicle sped up going downhill.

Suddenly, a deer jumped from the scrub oak into their path, darting away in a flash. Tires screeched and they both yelled, their cokes flying in the air, soaking their clothes and filling their laps with ice cubes. They both tore off their seatbelts, trying to swipe away the shocking cold, arms flailing about in a desperate attempt to help each other.

The curve came up fast. The jeep careened over the edge turning over and over. It tore the vegetation, hurtling through the ponderosa pine. They were both screaming as they were thrown from the jeep. Almost as suddenly as it had happened, the jeep—what was left of it—bumped to a stop at the bottom of the draw.

And then there was nothing but silence.

1

In Angel Fire, New Mexico, the new day always announced itself with shimmering gold atop the mountain, then the sun made a final push against the gray of dawn. The early workers and those who had trouble sleeping had become accustomed to it and would probably barely notice. When you saw it for the first time, it could take your breath away. At least, that's what Roberta Streit imagined as she watched the sun's path out of the bedroom window.

Roberta was at the stage of life when she noticed things like sunrises and sunsets, enjoyed them, and was thankful that she was still around to see them. She wasn't that old, of course, yet when one reached the age of retirement, one became more and more aware of matters like age and health. *Especially when people like your doctor and investment counselor looked like college kids,* Roberta thought.

Roberta glanced at the clock, then at her husband snuggled under the comforter. She smiled and climbed back into bed and curled up next to his warm body. He mumbled something incoherent.

"Go back to sleep. It's too early to get up," she whispered. She patted his shoulder and closed her eyes.

An hour and a half later, both Roberta and Al Streit stirred awake, rose and performed their morning routines with their usual dearth of conversation. Roberta slipped into a pair of jeans and an aqua tee shirt, brushed her brown hair (touched with gray, she had to admit), and headed out of the bedroom.

"Bye, Al," she called and blew a kiss to her husband as she walked through the living room toward the kitchen.

"So, you're headed to the Tuesday Morning Gossip Group?" he said, chuckling.

Roberta stopped and put her hands on her hips. "That is NOT our name, and you know it. We are the JULIETs. Besides, we don't gossip. We solve world problems."

"Sure, but you only have that name because we men are the ROMEOs, Retired Old Men Eating Out."

"Remember our proper name from now on, please—Just Us Ladies Indulgently Eating Together." She scooped up the car keys and her purse and headed toward the door.

"Bye," he called. "Are you coming back right after breakfast?"

"I plan to, unless Kay needs to run an errand. I never know."

Roberta—Bertie to her friends—headed down the mountain and around the curve, pulling into the driveway at Kay's log home, which was one of the prettiest in Angel Fire, Roberta believed, not only because it fit so well in the mountains, but also because it was so beautifully landscaped with natural wildflowers. She knew Kay spent a lot of time keeping everything weeded and orderly looking. Roberta, herself, loved the natural look of most of the yards in Angel Fire. Her natural yard, though, was a lot more . . . well, natural looking.

She watched as Kay came down the steps wearing white Capri pants and a royal blue knit top. Kay, petite with neatly cut gray hair and bright green eyes, always looked well put-together, and today was no exception in spite of her having a slumped and dejected look.

Kay slid into the passenger seat with only a mumbled hello. Before starting the car, Roberta looked at her companion. "What's wrong, Kay?" she asked.

"Nothing."

"Something is wrong," Roberta insisted. "Your eyes are red. You've been crying, haven't you?"

Kay sighed deeply. "Please, I don't want to talk about it."

"Are Heather and her family OK?" Roberta asked with a concerned frown.

"They're all fine," was the abrupt reply.

"Is it about Ed? Did you two have a fight?" Ed Wilson and Kay had been seeing a lot of each other over the past year, and Roberta had been glad that Kay had someone to fill the empty place in her life since her husband's death.

"No," Kay shook her head. "We didn't have a fight. Come on. Let's get to breakfast. The girls will wonder where we are."

Without a word Roberta shifted into gear and backed out of the drive.

As the two women entered the Expresso Cafe the bustle of the breakfast crowd bubbled up around them. The smell of freshly brewed coffee and sizzling bacon filled the air. They made their way to the three tables pushed together where their friends were gathering. Annabelle, with her straw hat, delicate pink eyelet blouse and matching pressed slacks, was already seated with her flowered cane propped beside her. She smiled a welcome, her bright red lipstick stark against her pale skin as she sat, hands folded, waiting patiently for everyone else to finish their greetings and settle in their seats.

Roberta looked around the table after they had all placed their breakfast orders. She became aware of the settling of the air around them as if life fell into place when this group of friends gathered every Tuesday morning to break bread together —a kind of communion. *Sometimes the most common everyday occurrences could become the most special,* Roberta thought. She turned to the younger woman sitting next to her and said, "Tessa, have you already run your miles or are you going after breakfast?"

Setting down her herbal tea Tessa replied, "No, Jim said he'd hike with me today so we'll go later and take Wilbur."

"Wilbur," scoffed Myra, pushing her thick glasses up on her nose. "What kind of name is that for a dog?"

"It's a perfectly good name, I'll have you know." Tessa understood Myra well enough by now not to take offense at what she said. Myra Stanhope was known throughout town for her outspokenness. She considered everyone's business her own, although she was always ready with a helping hand—especially one that held a casserole—if anyone needed help.

"Where's Olivia? Is she coming today?" asked Roberta.

"Oh, you know Livie," said Myra. "She's always late. What else can you expect from an artist?"

The friends all smiled, knowing how true that was about their friend.

"Did you hear there was a bad accident up by the pass late yesterday?" said Annabelle.

They all leaned forward, shaking their heads.

"I don't really know any details. A car went off the road at that bad curve. Two people were hurt or maybe killed, I don't know."

Expressions of concern were uttered by all, as Olivia rushed in and sat with them. "What are you talking about?" she asked breathlessly.

"An accident. At the pass. Did you hear anything about it?"

Olivia shook her head. "Kay, you went to Taos yesterday. Did you see anything?"

"No, I didn't see any trace of an accident. It must have happened after I went by." She took a quick sip of her coffee.

"Oh, did you go to Taos with Ed?" asked Myra.

"No," snapped Kay. "Why is everyone asking me about Ed today?"

"Well, excuse me for living," exclaimed Myra. "I knew you and Ed sometimes did things together so naturally I thought . . . "

"Well, don't always think that everything I do is with Ed," interrupted Kay. "I have a life of my own, you know."

Fortunately, their breakfasts arrived at that moment so that as dishes were directed to the right places, the moment's tension evaporated.

"I have to tell you the cutest thing that Elizabeth did," said Roberta, smearing jam on her toast."

"And, of course, Elizabeth would be one of your multitude of grandchildren?" said Myra.

Roberta smiled. "Yes, she's Jason's middle child. She's six now. She's the one who learned to ski at our great Children's Ski School. She was lucky and had Valerie Byrd and Lynn Coulam as instructors and she learned SO fast! Now her mom has trouble keeping up with her. Anyway, Jason sent me this cute video. Elizabeth had written a song and she sang it for me. It's 'I love you. You love me. We all love each other because we're family.' Isn't that so dear?"

Everyone smiled and nodded except Myra. "I think that's already a song, Bertie."

"Oh, well. I still thought it was cute."

Annabelle smiled her understanding. "Have any of you heard how that sweet young woman, Hannah, is doing?"

"Hannah?" asked Myra.

"You know. Her husband left her some months ago. She has a daughter, Shandra, a really nice girl, who's a senior here at Moreno Valley High School. Hannah didn't want to have to move back to her parents in Texas since it was Shandra's senior year."

Tessa nodded. "Yes, Sherry Sullivan got Hannah a job cleaning houses for the property managing arm of the realty company she works for. Sherry handles all that property managing stuff."

"That's nice," said Myra. "Maybe I should take them a casserole."

Roberta glanced at Tessa as a smile played across both their faces. "Why don't you let me check on her first? I'll let you know if they need a casserole, OK."

"Not to change the subject, but I read a distressing thing recently," commented Tessa. "Do you realize that every corn and wheat product in our country is a GMO?"

"What's a GMO?" asked Annabelle.

"Genetically Modified Organism. It's what the companies do to make it possible to grow more, make it last longer, have a longer shelf life and all that. Honestly, it's so hard to find anything that is truly organic anymore."

Conversations wove among the friends from one topic to another, from books they were reading, to village activities, recipes, aches and pains, and on and on. It formed a tapestry—from underneath it might look like a lot of loose threads, though on the other side it formed a picture of their friendship; it's what held them together in this small mountain community.

As they went their separate ways that morning, they were all aware of Kay's sadness and wished they could help.

And they wondered about the accident, hoping no one they knew had been involved.

"Need to run any errands before we go home?" Roberta asked before starting the car.

"No," was the curt reply from Kay.

Roberta shrugged, turned the key and put the car in gear. They rode in silence all the way to Kay's driveway.

Pulling to a stop, Roberta turned to her friend and tried one more time. "Look, Kay, it's obvious something happened to make you sad or mad. You know it always helps to talk about things that are on your mind. I'm your friend. I'm here to listen."

Kay's gaze finally met Roberta's, and tears started to well up on the edges of her eyes. "I know you're a friend I can talk to. It's only . . . I'm not ready to talk about it yet. I shouldn't have gone this morning. I simply need to be alone for a while." She patted Bertie's arm, opened the door, and scooted out of the car and into her house.

I think being alone is the last thing you need, Roberta thought as she backed out of the driveway and headed home. One of life's important lessons that Roberta had learned over the years was the importance of the support of friends, and how women can pull together to nurture and help each other. Through those early years of the adjustments of marriage, her two miscarriages, the raising of four children, the moves, and many more of life's events, big and small, it had been the sharing with a close woman friend that had been so meaningful.

Roberta's husband, Al, was exactly as she had left him, in his recliner with his feet propped up, reading the Albuquerque paper and watching CNN.

"Anything new?" he called out when Roberta walked into the kitchen.

She came into the room and sat on the denim slipcovered couch. "There was an accident yesterday evening, somewhere in the pass. No one had any details, though."

He lowered the paper. "Really? I thought I heard sirens. Hope it wasn't too bad."

"Me, too. Well, it will be all over the valley before long so we'll hear about it soon enough." She stood up and walked into their bedroom. Dropping her purse on the bed, she sat down beside it. *What in the world is wrong with Kay? She is obviously upset. I know it must involve Ed. She's been lonely for so long, and he really has brightened up her life.* She sighed deeply.

Roberta pushed herself up and ambled back into the great room where the sun was pouring through the huge windows. She straightened some magazines on the oak coffee table and looked around the room. She had fallen in love with this house the first time she had seen it. After walking in the front door that day, her gaze had lifted to the twenty-foot high pine ceiling of the great room which had a two-sided fireplace dividing the living and dining areas. Now that she had filled the house with their things: denim sofa and love seat, Al's recliner, end tables with family pictures, and bookcases filled with books. It suited her perfectly with the warm, cozy atmosphere she wanted.

"What are you going to do today?" asked Al, lowering his paper.

"Oh, I've got some gardening I want to do and . . . " The ringing of the phone interrupted their conversation.

"I'll get it," Al said reaching for the phone beside him. Looking at caller ID, he passed the phone to Roberta. "It's Myra," he announced. "Didn't you have breakfast with her a few minutes ago? She must have some new gossip."

"Hi, Myra," said Roberta, making a face at her husband as he smiled at her.

"Oh, Bertie, it's so awful!"

"What's awful?"

"I learned about the accident. It was Sherry. Sherry Sullivan. And you won't believe this. Guess who was with her?"

"I couldn't guess, Myra. Simply tell me."

"It was Ed Wilson. Kay's Ed—only he isn't Kay's anymore, I guess. And he was killed, Bertie. He's dead!"

2

"Oh, my God! No!" exclaimed Roberta. Roberta saw the concerned look on her husband's face and the question in his expression and quickly mouthed, "Ed Wilson died in that accident."

"Do you think that was what was wrong with Kay this morning?" asked Myra.

Roberta frowned. "No, that's not possible. If she had known, she would have said so. And she would have been a lot more upset. What about Sherry? Was she hurt?"

"Oh, yes. They were both thrown from the car. She was airlifted to UNM Hospital in Albuquerque from Taos after they took her to Holy Cross."

"Oh, my gosh. This is so hard to believe and so sad. I'll be anxious to hear how Sherry is doing. She's always been such a friendly person and a hard worker."

"And a man-stealer," added Myra.

"Myra! You don't know anything about their relationship."

"No, not yet."

"I bet that is what Kay was so upset about. She must have known Ed was seeing someone else."

"You're probably right," Myra agreed.

"You know," said Roberta, 'I'd better go over there and tell her about the accident and about Ed. It would be awful for her to find out when she was alone."

"Right. She'll be pretty upset." Myra paused. "Do you think I should take over a casserole? I have a couple of those ham, rice, and broccoli ones in my freezer ready to go."

Roberta rolled her eyes. "No, I don't think she needs a casserole right now. Maybe some other time. Let me get over there. Thanks for letting me know." After their good-byes, Roberta hung up the phone and related the details to her husband.

"How does that woman always have the latest scoop?" Al asked, shaking his head.

Roberta smiled. "I don't know. She always does . . . and it always is correct." She shook her head. "I hate to have to tell Kay, but I'd better get to it." She leaned over and kissed her husband on his forehead, and he patted her arm, the small communications of a long marriage that speak the words that are often left unsaid.

The short drive to Kay's house went too quickly. Pulling into Kay's driveway, Roberta turned off the ignition and sat for a moment staring ahead, wondering what words she should use. The iridescent blue of a Steller jay caught her eye as it flew from one pine tree to another. If she had hoped for inspiration from that she didn't get any.

Well, sitting here won't make it any easier. She swung her legs out of the car and approached the door. As she raised her hand to knock, the door opened.

"I heard someone drive up," Kay said, "so I looked out the window and saw you coming. I told you I was OK, I only wanted some time alone."

Roberta looked at her friend and shook her head. "I know. It's not that. I came because I need to tell you something."

"What is it?" A worried expression crossed her face. "Are you all right?"

"It's not me. Can I come in?"

Kay stood back and motioned Roberta in. "Of course. Come in. Let's go sit in the kitchen. Do you want a cup of coffee?"

"No, thanks," Roberta said, trying to smile. They walked through the high ceilinged living room with the huge stone fireplace that took up one wall. The other walls were all filled with large southwestern pieces of art. The sofa and chairs were of a warm brown tone with accent pillows of Native American patterns in turquoise and terra cotta, and large pottery pieces decorated the coffee- and end-tables. Sliding glass doors opened onto an inviting deck, but the two women moved through to the kitchen table where they had spent untold hours over the years.

"Well?" asked Kay, waiting expectantly.

Roberta sighed deeply. "I don't know any easy way to tell you this, Kay. A few minutes ago I learned that it was Ed in that accident yesterday."

"Ed?" Kay's hand flew to her mouth.

"Yes. And I hate to have to tell you," Roberta paused, looked toward the ceiling then made herself face Kay, "but . . . but he was killed."

"No!" With the single word, Kay jumped up, her chair flipping over in her haste. She turned and walked to the window. With her arms folded around her waist, she bent her head to the glass and whispered "No," over and over.

Roberta felt tears pooling in her own eyes. She rose and righted Kay's chair, then walked to her friend and put her arms around her. "I'm sorry. I'm so sorry."

"I can't believe it."

"I know. It's hard to take in," Roberta said. The two stood at the window as the reality sank in. After some moments, Kay straightened up and turned.

"I need a tissue," she said, moving to the kitchen counter and pulling a tissue box toward her. With several tissues in her hand, she went and sat again at the table.

"How did it happen?" she finally asked.

Roberta sat opposite her. "I don't know yet. I only heard that there was an accident, and Ed and Sherry Sullivan were thrown from the car. He was killed and Sherry has been airlifted to UNM Hospital."

"Sherry!" Kay spat out the name. "I knew he was seeing Sherry now." She looked up at Roberta. "I saw them together in Taos yesterday. That's why I was so upset this morning."

Roberta nodded. "I understand."

"Do you? Can you really understand when you still have your husband?" Her words sounded bitter. "Can you really understand what it has been like to have been alone for years and then think you might have found companionship again, only to have . . . to have . . . ," she stopped and buried her head in her arms on the table.

Silence filled the space around them for a few heartbeats.

Roberta reached across the table and put her hand gently on Kay's arm. "Maybe I can't completely understand, but I care enough about you to imagine how you feel. And I know there are really no words I can say to comfort you, or to help you in this terrible time. I want you to know that I'm here for you. I can only be here for you."

The two friends sat that way as the bright New Mexico sun shone on them as if, perhaps, it was trying to defy in some way the darkness of grief. Outside the window, life went on as usual. The Chickadees and Nuthatches flitted to and from the bird feeder, a chainsaw buzzed in the distance, a rare puff of cloud interrupted the blue, blue sky.

Kay sat, elbows resting on the table, her face in her hands. Her sobs had quieted. She continued to stay that way, occasionally shaking her head, trying to deny the terrible truth that wouldn't go away.

Roberta remained quiet, thinking about how lives can change in a heartbeat; how at this time yesterday Kay was peacefully going about her errands in Taos. She remembered the time, so long ago now, when she had realized her happily-anticipated pregnancy was ending. Until that moment, she had been filled with the feeling of joyous expectation, of becoming a family instead of only a couple, had imagined holding the warm, sweet smell of a baby close to her. Then the sudden, stabbing words of the doctor, taking her breath away, taking her dreams away. So cruel. That had been years and years ago, yet here, in this moment, she could feel the pain again. That is what Kay had ahead of her, that ambushing of grief, over and over when you least expect it. Roberta sighed, wishing there might be something she could do to lessen Kay's sadness, yet knowing there was nothing.

Roberta finally rose and began making coffee. As she placed the steaming cup by Kay, Kay sat up in her chair and wiped her eyes. "Thanks," she said softly.

Roberta simply patted Kay's shoulder and brought a cup for herself to the table.

"I know I didn't have any claim to Ed," Kay began. She took a sip of coffee. "He never said he loved me. Never talked about a future together. It's only that we seemed to like the same things. We enjoyed doing things together, you know?" She looked at Roberta and the pain in her eyes brought a lump to Roberta's throat. Roberta simply nodded.

"I think it started last summer at the first Music from Angel Fire concert. We happened to be sitting next to each other and we visited a little before the concert. Of course, we'd known each other from different things around town. It was a great concert." Kay smiled weakly, remembering. "I was the first to jump to my feet for a standing ovation at the end, and he was right there with me. He smiled at me —I'll never forget that smile—and said, 'You must be a girl after my own heart'" Kay chuckled. "'A girl,' he said. Imagine that? We spent the rest of the evening together." Kay shook her head. "It seemed so right between us. Whether it was golfing, or hiking, or eating out, or one of us cooking for the other, then watching some movie from Netflix, it was always fun."

They sat in silence, sipping their coffee.

"I didn't even realize at first that we were seeing less and less of each other. I merely thought he was busy, or I didn't think about it at all. Then, yesterday, I was in Taos and I saw them together." Tears filled Kay's eyes again, and she swiped them away with a tissue. "I couldn't finish my errands. I came right home. I felt . . . I felt . . ."

Roberta reached across the table and covered Kay's hand with her own. "You felt betrayed," she said.

Kay nodded. "Yes," she said. "Betrayed."

After their second cups of coffee, both Kay and Roberta had all the coffee they could stand for the day. As they rose to move out to the deck, there was a loud knock at the front door.

"Who could that be?" said Kay.

"Do you want me to get it?" asked Roberta.

Kay nodded, and Roberta went to the front door. Kay followed her inside as far as the kitchen door. Roberta soon returned with Myra, Annabelle, and Olivia in tow, each carrying a bag.

Myra pushed her way to the front, her stocky form encased in a purple warm-up suit. "We're all so sorry to hear about Ed. We knew you wouldn't be thinking about lunch, but you need to eat, so we brought lunch to you. Earlene made up your favorite chicken pesto wrap from the grill at the club, and we've got sandwiches for all of us and drinks, too."

Kay looked from one to the other, speechless.

"So, where shall we eat?" asked Myra. "Let's go out on the deck. It's a beautiful day." She herded the group ahead of her as Kay and Roberta exchanged a quick look and shook their heads. "Come on," Myra called over her shoulder. "Tessa was still hiking so I couldn't reach her, but your friends are here. This is a time for friends, after all."

At first, the usually vocal group was quiet, avoiding talk as they divided up the food and helped themselves to the drinks. They settled around the table on Kay's deck, shaded by the tall ponderosa pines. The warm June sunlight danced between the branches making patterns of light and shade. The house bordered on green space, and the group waved to Sharron Harris and Melanie Mantooth as the two were hiking the trail that wound its way through the woods.

Olivia looked around as she set down her grilled cheese sandwich. "Kay, have you ever realized how perfect the lighting is at your house for painting? You could have a wonderful studio here if you wanted."

Kay shook her head. "I've never painted, and that's something I will probably never do." Trying to carry on a normal conversation, to make small talk, took a huge effort for Kay. She felt that she was outside this place, watching these people talk and eat as if acting in a play. Nothing felt real to her.

"Tessa and I went through one of the galleries in Taos a few weeks ago, and she told me a funny story," Annabelle said. "She said she had wanted to try oil painting with a friend. They took a class, and she really loved it. She decided to paint a small landscape for her father for Father's Day, a snow scene, I think. When he opened the package, he said to her, 'Is this one of those paint-by-number things?'"

The group laughed, and even Kay managed a small smile.

"That was the last time she painted anything," Annabelle added.

Olivia nodded. "She's told me that story, too. I wish she'd try again. Honestly, that father of hers is something else."

"Isn't it a shame when some small comment by a parent or teacher or someone can discourage us from trying things?" Roberta shook her head. "I don't think I was as aware of that with my four kids, though I certainly am with my grandkids."

Myra snorted. "You and your grandkids! I don't know how you keep them all straight."

"I don't have any problem with that, Myra. Besides, even though you have only two grandchildren, dear friend, I notice that you are as fiercely proud of them and involved with their lives as I am with mine."

Myra managed a wry grin as she pushed her glasses back up on her nose.

"Speaking of how words might be discouraging," Annabelle went back to the previous comment. "It is amazing, the power of words, especially when we are young. In my little high school in the small town I grew up in before my family moved to Dallas, everyone was in the school chorus, so, of course, I was too. When it came time for concerts, the director asked me to mouth the words. I guess I was throwing everyone off. To this day, when we sing at church or anything, I try to sing softly so that no one will hear me."

"Oh, poor Annabelle!" exclaimed Roberta.

"I can't imagine you in a small town, Annabelle," said Olivia. "You are so 'Dallas', so sophisticated, so big city."

"Well, I do love Dallas, and love being there part of the year," admitted Annabelle, "but I also love Angel Fire, and this is definitely not a big city." This was greeted with nods and smiles all around.

Roberta sat back and watched her friends as conversation scattered from one subject to another, yet never touching the one thing that was on everyone's mind. She noticed that while Kay said nothing, at least this visit seemed to keep her grief at bay—if only for the moment.

3

Roberta finally returned home in the mid-afternoon, only to find a note from Al that he was at the driving range. She breathed in the silence of the house. Roberta usually found it comforting. For some reason today it made her feel lonely and sad. *I don't know what I would do if something happened to Al,* she thought. She wandered out to the deck and checked the birdfeeders, which Al must have filled before he left.

She settled on the blue and white striped cushions of the most comfortable chair, which glided gently back and forth. The air smelled clean and fresh with the lingering scent of pine and of the petunias in a planter by her chair. The only sounds were the soft creak of the chair's movement, the chatter of a squirrel scolding her, and the breeze moving softly through the trees. She sighed with contentment, a feeling she usually had when she relaxed on the deck. As often happened at times like this, her thoughts turned to the quirks of fate that had brought them to live in Angel Fire, New Mexico.

Al had been an engineer with a computer company he had started in California. They had come many times to the Santa Fe and Taos area, enjoying the artistic aspects, the cuisine, the whole ambiance of the City Different, as Santa Fe was called. One of their favorite things to do was to take drives, meandering on back roads, and even forest service roads, marveling at the scenery and peacefulness that would surround them.

Roberta would never forget the autumn day they happened to drive through a small farming area called Ocate, then followed the rough, hilly dirt road, climbing higher and higher. They passed through a lush valley with cattle grazing in the distance, continuing on, winding their way up around S-curves to another valley, then starting down again through golden aspens and ponderosa pines. As they came out of the trees, right before a 90-degree turn, Al pulled the car off the road and stopped. Before them lay a beautiful valley, a ranch in the distance and, straight ahead, a view of the snow-capped Wheeler Peak range of the Sangre de Cristos Mountains.

They sat for moments not saying a word, savoring the beauty, listening to the wind tremble through the aspens, shimmering in their fall mantle of gold.

"I want to live in this valley," Al's voice was almost a whisper, as if they were in a hallowed cathedral where they were awed into quietness.

Roberta pulled her gaze from the scene before her and turned to her husband. "It's a beautiful place," she admitted. "But how would you make a living?"

"Well, I don't know yet." He paused. "If I could find a way, would you be willing?"

"Let's look into this a little more before we make any decisions," she had said that day. Even then, she suspected that it was only a matter of time until they would be residents of northern New Mexico.

Roberta smiled as she remembered. It had only taken Al a year and a half to sell his company, get hired to upgrade the resort's computer systems, and find this house which they both fell in love with immediately. Then they had to convince their grown kids that they weren't having a mid-life crisis by moving to this small mountain community. After the grandkids had experienced the thrill of skiing and the freedom of a summer in the mountains of Angel Fire, all four of Roberta and Al's children had declared their parents were absolutely brilliant for moving to Angel Fire.

A hot air balloon appeared in Roberta's view, then another, like colorful exclamation points in the sky. *They must be getting ready for the Balloon Festival this weekend,* she thought. *I must be sure to get Kay to that. It would be fun, and I don't want to let her sit around grieving too much.* But how much was too much? Roberta had never figured that out. She'd heard people talk about widows and widowers, saying "It's been a year (or two years, or whatever) and they need to get on with their lives, put the sadness behind them." It seemed to her that a person's grief was like their shadow. The length and breadth of it changed from hour to hour, day to day, season to season, and it was simply part of you. You couldn't change it simply because you made up your mind to do that, or because someone said your shadow should be shorter. It was what it was, and you couldn't help it. Why were people so determined to think they knew what was best for someone else? She could never understand that. One needed to walk in another's shoes, as her mom had told her many times.

Roberta found that her thoughts had made her irritated, so she deliberately put them away and concentrated on the paths of the hot air balloons as they glided their way across the sky. Her gaze moved to watch a Chickadee snatch a sunflower seed from the feeder then fly off to the nearest tree. *I wonder how Kay is doing,* she thought. *Her dreams have ended so tragically. We've always been friendly with Sherry. How will Kay treat her now? This is a small town, and their paths will often cross.* She took a deep breath marveling, as usual, at the clean, fresh scent of the mountain air. The balloons slipped out of her view, carrying their bright red and yellow colors with them.

Kay finished rinsing the coffee cups from that morning and set them in the dish drainer to dry. The swish of warm, soapy water on her hands and the routine of chores had helped her to stay grounded, to touch the numbness that she felt all the way to the deepest part of her. She had the sense that she was like a balloon, tethered only by a feeble string, and that at any moment the string would loosen and she'd drift away. She wiped her hands on the tea towel, rehung it, and walked slowly back to her bedroom. Looking at her bed, she wanted to climb in and pull the covers over her head, even though she knew her tormented thoughts would keep her from any rest.

Instead, she sat in her favorite chair by the window and took up her Bible. She read the words beginning from where her reading had left off yesterday morning, but they were only words with no meaning for her now. So much had happened since she had last opened her Bible.

I've always found comfort in the Scriptures. What can they say to me to heal this broken heart, this terrible disappointment? I know there's something there for me, but right now I don't even care about looking for it.

She closed the Bible slowly and set it back on the table, picking up the latest novel she was reading, "Written in My Own Heart's Blood" by Diana Gabaldon, one of her favorite authors.

An hour later Kay was amazed to find that she had managed to lose herself in the book for a space of time. *I guess I'll find a way to go on living,* she thought ruefully. She stood and stretched and walked into the living room to turn on the cooking channel on the TV.

As she picked up the remote control her phone rang. Without thinking to check the caller ID, she answered. "Hello."

"Hello, Kay. This is Myra."

Kay felt herself grimace. "Hi, Myra."

"I've got this nice casserole. Would you like me to bring it over for your dinner?"

"Myra," Kay struggled to keep the anger out of her voice. "That's kind of you, I'm sure, but I don't need a casserole. I'm not sick. I haven't had any surgery. I'm fine."

"I know you are. You don't have to get mad about it. I was only trying to be neighborly."

Kay sighed. "I know, and it is thoughtful of you. Still I think it's better if you keep the casseroles for when they're really needed."

"Well, if you're sure. Will you please call me if you need anything?"

"I will, Myra. I promise. Thanks."

They said their goodbyes and Kay hung up the phone, shaking her head. Whenever Myra mentioned having a *nice* casserole, Kay always had the desire to say she'd rather have one of the *naughty* ones. So far, though, she had managed to hold her tongue. She plumped up the couch pillows, sat down and clicked on the cooking channel.

Myra drummed her fingers on the phone after she had placed it back in its cradle. It was obvious that Kay was really hurting over Ed's death, or maybe it was more about Ed having been with Sherry. Myra wanted to do something to help her, to fix things. Beyond offering a casserole, she really didn't know what to do. She sighed and walked through her kitchen to the garage. Opening the freezer, she counted the casseroles she had ready and waiting. Six in all. She was in the mood to make up a new batch, but six was a lot to have on hand. Maybe she should make up some cookies to take to the United Church of Angel Fire for the fellowship time after church. They always needed cookies at the United Church.

In fact, Myra thought with a sense of excitement, *they will need cookies for Vacation Bible School, and for the Fun Nights for the middle and high schoolers.* She found herself smiling as she assembled the ingredients to make cookies. She tied an apron around her rather large waist, and brought the eggs from the refrigerator to the counter. For the next hour, she lost herself in mixing up several kinds of cookies and sliding the shiny cookie sheets in and out of her two ovens.

Myra would never want her friends to know, but she so often felt lost and alone in her house, a house that was always too big for them, even before her husband had died. It was the house he had wanted, and she really couldn't see any point in going through all the trouble of selling it and finding something smaller. It even had that whole apartment on the lower level which she kept closed off. Once, Sherry had suggested she rent it out, but who knew what kind of people would be coming and going, so she had refused. Still, she sometimes thought it might be nice to hear someone else around. The silence could be a lonely echo throughout the house.

Now, though, she was doing what she loved best—doing something for others, as her mother had always told her was the most important thing to do. "If you're not doing for others," her mother would say, "you might as well be dead." That had seemed a little harsh to Myra as a child, but she had loved and admired the somewhat aloof personage of her mother, whose days were filled with club and community activities, so she believed it must be true. At any rate, she was enjoying herself now, surrounded by the scents of chocolate and cinnamon. She hummed an old tune as the sun made its way across the sky.

The policeman and state trooper walked in widening circles from the place the jeep—or what was left of it—finally ended up. The dried leaves and pine needles crunched under foot. The air was cool and still in this lower part of the mountain, the pines making a canopy overhead, holding the sun at bay.

"I haven't seen any evidence of open alcoholic beverages, have you?"

"Nope. Nothing."

"So, what do you think happened?" asked the rookie Angel Fire policeman, a recent transfer from Kansas. He wasn't surprised by the accident. In his short time in Angel Fire he had heard about and witnessed some crazy driving on the road between Angel Fire and Taos. Combine that with the curvy road and mountain terrain and he expected accidents every day. He was still adjusting to the change from flat wheat fields to what he found in the Sangre de Cristos.

The state trooper had seen this kind of accident a number of times. "From the skid marks, I believe something, probably a deer, jumped in front of them."

"Do you think they hit it?"

The trooper shook his head. "There's no sign of blood on the front of the jeep or in the road. Even so, we should hike in a little way on the other side of the road to be sure."

The policeman looked back up the steep incline and grimaced thinking about climbing up even more once they got back up to the road. "I can't imagine them not wearing seat belts. With a jeep this open, no top or sides, that was pretty foolish. No wonder they were thrown out."

"Yeah. There might be some explanation, though I don't know what it would be. It's not like they were thoughtless kids. Maybe when the lady is finally able to talk, we'll get some answers."

"When do you think that will be?" asked the policeman.

"Who knows?" The trooper shrugged his shoulders. "If she even makes it. She was in pretty bad shape, they said."

The younger man dusted off his uniform sleeve. "Maybe we'll never learn what really happened."

"Oh, I think we'll know eventually. It's like a puzzle we have to put together. You only need the one certain piece for the whole thing to become clear."

The two men took a final look around and began the long trudge back up to the road.

Kay turned off the TV and walked into the kitchen. She still had half of her chicken pesto wrap from lunch that would do for her supper. She filled a glass with water and started for the deck when her phone rang again. This time, she looked at the caller ID and seeing that it was her daughter, she answered quickly.

"How are you Mom?" Heather asked.

"Oh, I'm OK. How are you?"

"Mom? I can tell by your voice that something's wrong. What's happened? Are you sick?"

"Nothing like that. Actually, though, I've had a bad day. There was a car accident on the pass yesterday and Ed Wilson was killed." She felt annoyance at herself that tears were starting again.

"Ed Wilson? That guy you went places with?"

"Yes. That one."

"Mom! You could have been with him! You might have been in that accident, too. Oh, my God!"

A cold chill went through Kay. "I . . . I never thought of that," she admitted. "He was with someone else, though. Someone I know well, Sherry Sullivan. Did you ever meet her when you were visiting?"

"No, I don't think so. Gosh, Mom, I'm so sorry. I know you must be sad about his death. What a shock." She paused. "Do you want me to come out this weekend?"

Kay smiled at her daughter's thoughtfulness. "No, honey, that's not necessary. I do feel stunned, of course. I'll be OK. I've got some good friends here. In fact, Myra has already offered me one of her casseroles."

Heather chuckled. "That sounds like Myra. But, Mom, what a terrible thing to happen. Was the lady killed, too?"

"No. She was badly hurt. They airlifted her to Albuquerque."

"Oh, Mom. I am so sorry. I know you enjoyed doing things with Ed, and we were glad for you. I know it's been hard since Dad died."

Kay found that she could only mumble, "Yes" through the lump in her throat.

"Maybe I should come up," Heather said. "Dick and the boys will understand."

"There's no need, Heather. Honestly. How are the boys? And Dick?"

"Everyone's fine. Keeping busy as always. The boys both have baseball practice this afternoon. Dick had to make a quick trip to Dallas for a meeting. He'll be back tonight. I'm glad it's summer and I'm off from school. It makes the logistics of getting the boys to their activities so much easier, even though Dick was out of town."

Kay always loved talking with Heather, but today even the effort of this conversation was weighing her down. "Good," said Kay quickly. "Well, give them my love. We'll talk again soon, all right?"

"All right, Mom. I love you."

"I love you, too, hon. Bye for now."

"Bye, Mom."

Kay looked down at the phone a moment after she had hung up. Then she sat at the kitchen table, buried her face in her hands and wept. The sound of her grief slipped into corners, slid up the walls, wrapped itself around everything until it filled the house.

4

Sherry Sullivan's only daughter, Amber, paced back and forth in front of the ICU, waiting for the next time she could go back in for a few minutes and stand helplessly by her mother's bed. She thought that she would never be able to erase the memory of the antiseptic smell, the constant beeping of the monitors, and the sight of her mother swathed in bandages and connected to all kinds of tubes. She checked her watch. Twenty-two more minutes before she could go back in. She went back to the waiting area, sank into the green vinyl chair and pulled out her cell phone.

Other people sat scattered around the ICU waiting area, some in soft conversation, others flipping endlessly through the tattered magazines left lying around. They were all strangers to each other, but bound together by a universal thread of the unusual bedfellows of fear, anguish, and hope. There was the woman who'd worn the same black slacks and green tee shirt for two days, who obviously hadn't left during that time; the man who stared ahead and chewed on his fingernails; the couple who vacillated between holding hands and snapping at each other. They would all nod to each other in the hospital cafeteria or, more often, at the vending machines around the corner. Amber flipped through the emails on her phone. Only sixteen more minutes.

Sherry felt like she was coming up out of a dark hole. She tried to open her eyes, but it was difficult. There was tremendous pain yet she couldn't focus on where it was. She tried blinking her eyes, cringing from the brightness around her.

"Oo-o-h," she murmured in protest.

Immediately, a friendly face came into view. "You're OK," it said. "Welcome back to the world."

Sherry definitely didn't feel OK, but she couldn't grasp what was wrong. "What . . . ? Where am I?" She felt so confused, she didn't even know what questions to ask. She only knew she needed some answers fast.

"You've been in an accident." The face mouthing the words blurred.

Sherry sensed the darkness closing in again. She heard beeping noises, and tried again to open her eyes.

"Tell me . . . " was all she managed to get out between her parched, swollen lips.

"You were in a car accident yesterday. You're in the ICU at UNM Hospital in Albuquerque. You've had surgery on your leg, arm and shoulder, and you had some injury to your head. It's important for you to stay quiet now. We're going to take good care of you. Your daughter is here. When you wake up again, we'll bring her in to see you."

Amber, Sherry thought. She wanted to say her daughter's name out loud, tell them to bring her in right now, but no words formed. Sherry's limbs were so heavy she couldn't move. Her eyes closed and there was nothing but the blackness again.

Although the area certainly needed the water, Roberta couldn't help but feel a little disappointed when she woke to cloudy skies on Tuesday.

"We're spoiled by all the sunshine we get here," Al commented as Roberta stood at the window watching the billowing clouds turning to a darker gray.

Roberta sighed. "It's only that an overcast day can make a person feel down, you know? I'm thinking about Kay. She doesn't need anything to make her feel any sadder than she already is."

Al walked up beside Roberta and put his arm around her, giving her a little squeeze. "Then I guess you'd better go and pick her up for your breakfast group and cheer her up, honey."

She turned to him, gave him a quick kiss on his cheek, and said, "OK. I'm off. See you after breakfast."

When Kay climbed in Roberta's car the first thing she said was, "I really didn't want to go to breakfast today, Bertie. I wish you hadn't talked me into it."

"I know," Roberta said and smiled at her friend. "But you need to go."

"I don't want everyone looking at me and feeling sorry for me. 'Poor old Kay. Ed dumped her for a younger woman.' And, really, I only want to be alone to grieve over Ed's death. I still can't believe it."

"It is hard to believe. I heard his son arranged for the body to go back to Texas where they had the funeral."

Kay nodded, pulled out a tissue and wiped her eyes. "I'll do better if we don't talk about it."

Roberta headed the car down the hill. "I bet everyone will be sensitive to your feelings and not bring it up."

Kay gave a little snort. "Everyone except Myra, maybe."

"If she starts, we'll all head her off. Simply ignore her." They pulled into a parking space near the Expresso Café. Roberta patted Kay's arm. "It'll be fine. Come on."

They were the last two of the group to gather at the tables. The others looked up and there was a brief second of silence before the usual greetings filled the air. As Kay and Roberta sat down, at least four different conversations continued around them.

Tessa seemed especially animated. "What are you talking about, Tessa?" asked Roberta.

"Oh, you all. You wouldn't believe the latest about my dad!" she exclaimed. The other conversations died down to hear.

"I've told you all about my dad, the crazy Sicilian." Nods all around. "Well, he's gotten kicked out of the latest retirement home he was in. My brother is frantically trying to get him in somewhere else."

"What happened? Why was he kicked out?"

"Oh, it's unbelievable! He had this girlfriend, Edith."

"A girlfriend?" questioned Myra. "Isn't he in his 90s?"

Tessa nodded. "Sure. He's 93. But remember, he's Sicilian."

The group laughed. "So," Tessa continued, "they would walk around all day, hand in hand, as happy as you please. You know, he's an extreme narcissist, and she was in a state of complete dementia, so they would spend the days, with him talking about how wonderful he was and her simply enjoying someone talking to her. They were a perfect couple. But then, my dad thought some other man was interested in Edith, so he started fighting with him."

"You don't mean actual fighting, like with hitting, do you?" Annabelle was incredulous.

"Yes. That's exactly what I mean."

"Oh, my gosh. That *is* unbelievable!" gasped Olivia.

"Unbelievable, but true," said Tessa, shaking her head, her long, brown pony tail bobbing.

"So, where is your dad now? Is your brother keeping him?"

"No, thank goodness," said Tessa. "He's been put in 'time out' in the geriatric psychiatric wing of the hospital, or whatever they call it. He can stay there for a little while so my brother can make some arrangements."

Annabelle looked around at the smiling faces of the group. "It sounds funny, but really that's sad, especially for and you and your brother, Tessa. I know you must both worry."

"Sure, but we're used to that kind of thing from him."

"Well, keep us posted," said Roberta.

Their breakfasts arrived and the friends took a few moments to refill coffee cups. "We're at that age of having these worries about our parents, aren't we?" said Olivia. "My mother and dad have an apartment in a retirement home and she told me the funniest story once. She and her friend Janet were walking down the hall when this really old guy, about a hundred-years-old, walked up and started talking to them. They knew him, of course. At the end of the conversation, he turned to Janet and said, 'Sometime, when you're alone, I want to ask you an important question. It's extremely important.' He emphasized that several times. Well, my mom and Janet puzzled about it for a few days, wondering what the important question could be. Finally, Janet saw the guy sitting alone in the lobby one day, so she went up to him and asked him what the question was that he had wanted to ask her. He looked at her with a blank expression and said 'Huh?' He didn't have a clue about the question, so they will never know."

"And neither will we. Honestly," complained Myra, "you shouldn't have aroused our curiosity. Now I'll wonder about that for the rest of my life."

After the laughter died down, Roberta commented that there were enough funny stories from retirement homes to make a sitcom.

"I thought maybe Wanda would get here this morning," said Olivia.

"Wanda Smith, you mean? I didn't think they were up here yet."

"I wasn't expecting them to get here until later," agreed Olivia, "but I thought I saw a light in their house on my way home last evening."

"Oh, I doubt it. Wanda usually lets us know exactly when she's coming." Annabelle pushed back her plate. Today she was dressed in a crisply ironed white blouse, blue linen slacks and, of course, her perky, little straw hat.

Olivia shrugged. "Well, maybe it was only the way my car lights shone on the window."

"I'll look at my emails when I get home and see if I've missed any from Wanda," Annabelle said.

Although Annabelle's husband was an avid golfer, Roberta often wondered how much longer they would continue to come up from Dallas. Annabelle seemed to need to rely more and more on her cane for getting around, and with no sidewalks except up to the hotel, walking around Angel Fire sometimes could be difficult. Several of the friends who used to come to the breakfast group from years past had moved on. Sometimes it was because the altitude of this approximately 8,500 foot high Sangre de Cristo mountain community had begun to bother them and sometimes because the births of grandchildren lured them closer to their families. At any rate, Roberta had always hated to see them go. *Am I getting so old that I'm afraid of change?* she wondered.

The Tuesday morning breakfast group ate and chatted their way through another morning, and Kay breathed a sigh of relief. As the friends left the café, the first splatters of rain began to fall.

"Good news," the nurse told Sherry. "We're moving you out of ICU to a private room this morning. Tomorrow you'll start some therapy."

Sherry could only give a wan smile. Amber had flown back to her job in Atlanta the day before, and Sherry was feeling terribly alone.

As if reading her mind, the nurse said, "You'll perk up in your own room, your friends can come and visit you."

"I don't know who'd come all the way from Angel Fire to see me," Sherry said. She tried to think who might make the trip. Maybe Steve, her boss at the real estate company. She'd had several phone calls, but hadn't been able to take them in the ICU. Perhaps talking to friends on the phone would help.

Sherry hadn't been settled in her room more than an hour when the state trooper showed up. He was a big man, tall and stocky, with dark hair and deep brown eyes. Simply his presence made Sherry feel intimidated. *Why did Amber have to leave for Atlanta so soon?* she anguished.

"I hate to bother you, Ms. Sullivan, but I've been the one investigating your accident and I need to ask you some questions. I'm Officer Thornton with the State Police." He pulled out a little pad from his pocket, then clicked open a pen.

Sherry nodded, but dreaded the conversation. Even though they had told her Ed was killed, she hadn't had to discuss it or even think about it. It was like a monster looming under the bed, and she wasn't ready to face that monster yet.

"We know you and Mr. Wilson were driving from Taos to Angel Fire, but which of you was driving, you or Mr. Wilson?"

Tears pooled in Sherry's eyes. "I . . . I can't remember. I don't remember anything about that day, or the accident. Nothing."

"Can you explain why neither of you were wearing seatbelts? Are you in the habit of going without a seatbelt?

"No! I always have my seatbelt on when I'm in a car. Always."

"So, you can't explain why you weren't wearing one that day?" He scowled at her while waiting for her answer.

"I told you. I remember nothing about that day. Nothing! Please believe me, Officer. I don't know why. I can't imagine not wearing a seatbelt." Sherry shook her head in frustration. "I truly don't remember anything."

"Your doctor told us there was some amnesia from that day, but maybe if you really tried to go back in your mind you might remember some detail. Where had you been in Taos that day?"

The tears escaped and slid down her face. She raised her hand that didn't have the IV attached and swiped them quickly away. "I keep telling you, I don't remember anything about that day. Honestly, I'm telling you the truth, Officer."

His eyes looked at her sternly from under his dark eyebrows. "I understand that even though the jeep belonged to Mr. Wilson, you often drove it."

"I . . . well, yes, I did drive it sometimes. It was fun to drive."

The officer made a note in his little pad.

"But I don't know if I was driving that day or not." Her voice sounded a little frantic, even to her own ears. Was she driving? She had no idea, and didn't want to think about that possibility. "Please," she said. "Please, don't keep asking me. I don't know anything about that day. I simply don't know." Sherry felt her heart beating faster.

The officer stood quietly for a moment, tapping his pen against the pad. "OK. We'll leave it at that for now. But if you remember anything, anything at all, please call this number." He scratched a number on the bottom of the paper and tore it from the pad, handing it to her.

Sherry nodded. After the door swung shut behind him, she leaned back against her pillows and let the tears flow.

She did not want to think about what had happened that day, the day that was erased completely from her mind. She didn't want to face the fact that Ed had died . . . and that she might have been responsible.

5

Tessa and Jim hiked along the Elliott Barker trail, occasionally exchanging comments, but mostly walking in silence as was their custom. Tessa led, her long brown ponytail swinging with each step, her strides even and strong. The sounds of the forest moved gently around them: the wind through the leaves, the birds chirping, the soft crunch of their hiking boots on the dry pine straw. Jim had removed Wilbur's leash, and the dog bounded up and back along the trail, never letting too much distance grow between him and his owners.

Tessa stopped and looked at Jim as he caught up with her.

"What's the matter?" he asked.

"Would you mind . . . ?" she began. "Could we go up to where Ed and Sherry's accident was?"

"Why would you want to do that?"

She shrugged. "I don't know. I . . . I kind of feel like I'd like to look around a little. It was such a terrible accident, and there are still so many unanswered questions."

"And you don't think the police are capable of handling it without you?" he asked, a knowing grin on his face.

"You know that's not it. I'm curious, that's all."

"OK. I can see you're determined. Lead the way."

She gave her husband a quick smile and started off at a brisk pace.

As Tessa approached the accident site she felt a strange uneasiness, as if she was treading where she should not be. She looked around at the wounded earth, the small saplings torn and thrown down, the bigger trees nicked and scraped, the underbrush gone. The wrecked jeep had been removed, although Tessa could still see its path down the mountainside. She shuddered, imagining those moments for Ed and Sherry.

Jim walked a short way to the side, slipped to the ground and leaned his back against a ponderosa pine. Tessa moved slowly around the accident site, noting the profusion of footprints already there. *Looks like the police did a thorough job,* she thought. She started up the steep incline, following the scarred earth. She wasn't sure why she had wanted to do this or what she was looking for. Perhaps because they were the same age, she was a closer friend of Sherry's than the others in the Tuesday morning group. She planned to visit Sherry in the hospital later that week when she and Jim had errands to do in Albuquerque. She wanted to get a clear picture of everything for Sherry's sake, and this seemed like an important starting place.

Tessa followed the rough trail made by the jeep's descent and made her way to the top where the tow truck must have been situated as it lowered cables to haul the jeep up. She stopped and looked around. She lowered herself to the ground and sat for a moment, trying to picture the event as it must have unfolded. She knew how flimsy Ed's old jeep was. Why didn't they have their seat belts on? Tessa shook her head at the foolishness of it. She couldn't imagine anyone as practical as Sherry not wearing her seatbelt.

She sighed and put her hands on the ground to push herself up. Her fingers touched something odd-feeling, something not natural for that place. Looking down, she gasped as her hand brushed over a smattering of white pills. Tessa glanced quickly at Jim. His eyes were closed as he rested against the tree. She scooped up the pills and slipped them into the pocket of her hiking shorts. *What could this mean? Does this have anything to do with the accident? How could the police have missed this?* She had never considered that alcohol might play a part in the accident. Could whoever was driving been on some drug? She should probably turn the pills in to the police, but she would talk to Sherry first. She stood quickly and tried to put this out of her mind as she worked her way back to her husband. Somehow, the peacefulness she always felt hiking this forest trail had been replaced with a vague uneasiness.

"I brought this get well card for you all to sign for Sherry," Tessa announced the next day at the Tuesday morning breakfast gathering. "Jim and I are going to Albuquerque Thursday and I'll stop by and see Sherry." She passed the card and pen to Annabelle.

"Has anybody heard any more about the investigation," Olivia asked. They all looked at Myra, their constant source of news.

"Not much," Myra said. "Evidently, Sherry remembers nothing about the accident, so the police can only piece together what happened. It started because a deer probably jumped out in front of them and they swerved. Why they didn't have seat belts on is a mystery. They seem to think that Ed, or whoever was driving, couldn't regain control, overcorrected or something, and they went over the side at that worst possible place."

"Such a shame," said Annabelle as she passed the card on to Kay after writing a short note. Roberta noticed that Kay's mouth formed a tight line as she held the card for a moment, sighed, then dashed off a quick message and handed it on to Olivia.

"Jim and I hiked the Elliott Baker Trail yesterday, and I saw where the accident happened."

Everyone stopped eating and stared at Tessa. Kay put her hands in her lap, gripping them together.

"Well, what did it look like?" asked Olivia. "Was the jeep still there?"

"Oh, no, it was gone. You could tell where it had been, its path down the mountain. It all looked . . . so terribly, terribly sad." Tessa took a sip of her tea. As the silence hung over them, she was sorry she had even mentioned it.

Myra pushed her plate forward after her last bite, ready to give out more information about the goings-on in the valley. "Did you hear about the bear that tore apart Becky Jones' house and almost got inside?" She glanced around with satisfaction seeing that she had everyone's attention.

"Well, tell us," urged Olivia. "What happened?"

"I heard this from Curtis himself," began Myra, as if she needed to show off her authenticity. "Becky wasn't home, maybe off doing something to get ready for Music from Angel Fire or the United Church of Angel Fire. Anyway, Curtis was working in his office and he had the feeling someone was watching him. He glanced at the window and there was this big bear on the deck, looking at him through the window. Of course, he made lots of noise to scare the bear off, then he went back to work. All of a sudden, he heard this huge grating noise from outside the house. He ran out on the deck and saw the bear pulling the siding off his house by the kitchen wall. He jumped around and yelled and the bear ran off."

"Oh, my gosh!" exclaimed Roberta. "Was that bear trying to get in their house and get to Curtis or what?"

"Curtis thinks the bear smelled some melon rinds that were in their trash right inside the wall the bear was tearing at. Probably, the bear was only hungry."

"How scary to have a bear tearing your house apart!" said Annabelle.

Myra nodded. "Curtis said that bear tore off about ten feet of siding."

Comments commiserating with the Jones' and then further bear stories—everyone had one—filled up most of the breakfast time. Of course, there was also the usual passing around of books read and enjoyed. Tessa looked around at the others. Should she say something about the pills she found? Ask what she should do with them? No, she decided. It would be best to talk to Sherry first.

While they had been having breakfast, a typical mountain storm had billowed up over the valley. Glancing up before she and Kay dashed to the car, Roberta yelled, "I guess this is what we should expect now that it's our 'monsoon season'" They jumped in the car without getting too wet. Roberta glanced over at Kay as she started up the car. "I'm glad you signed that card for Sherry," she said. "I can imagine what you wanted to say."

Kay gave a little snort. "My mother raised me right, so I simply wished her a speedy recovery."

Roberta smiled and soon pulled into Kay's driveway. She turned to her friend. "How are you doing, Kay?"

Kay shrugged as tears came to her eyes. "I'm OK. I'm grieving, that's for sure. I'm so confused about what to grieve about. If Ed hadn't died, I'd be sad about losing him as such a close companion; yet since I saw him with Sherry I'd already lost him. Oh, I don't know, Bertie. I feel sad on so many levels!"

"It makes it complicated, I'm sure. The bottom line is you need to grieve and your friends are here to help you when you need them."

"I know. I know. When Tessa mentioned about seeing the accident site, I thought I would die. Every time I think of it, I feel like my heart is breaking all over again. It's only . . . Bertie, I'm so angry! I'm so mad at Sherry and at Ed, too. Why? Why couldn't he let me know so I didn't find out that way?"

Roberta shook her head and remained silent. Sometimes, there are simply no words.

The rain drummed on the car, and the windows steamed up, making the inside into a cozy cave. The two friends sat in companionable silence for a few moments. Kay sighed and, staring out the fogged-up window, began, "Who knew life could have these bumps in the road? We go along, day by day, so busy and caught up in our routine, in our families, our working and cooking and cleaning and socializing and church, and we think that's what life is all about. Then something like this happens, and we realize all the rest is nothing. Nothing, Bertie." She turned toward her friend. "Life is what happens when you get socked in the stomach so hard that you have to work at getting your next breath. You have to figure out how to go on when everything changes."

Roberta gave a tender smile, and shrugged. "No, it's all life, Kay. All of it."

Kay looked at her hands, then looked up at Roberta. "I guess so." She paused. "I'd sure like to get back to the nothing part of it, the routine of every day."

"You'll get there. It will take time. In the meantime, try to keep busy. You know the Balloon Festival will be here this weekend. That's always fun to see, even if we can't begin to compare to Albuquerque's world-famous event. Let's go to the mass ascension on Saturday. I'll call and tell you what time we'll pick you up."

Kay shook her head, but smiled. "You're impossible. OK, I'll go. Thanks."

"And Al and I are going to dinner at the club on Friday night. Why don't you come with us? Marcie Klinger will be playing the piano there that night, and you know how everyone loves that."

"You're a good friend, Bertie, the best. I'll go to the balloon festival with you, but I'm not ready to go to the club yet."

Roberta nodded. "OK. I'll accept that."

Kay pulled her umbrella from her purse and turned to go. With her hand on the door handle, she paused. "Thanks," she murmured. She turned back to Roberta. "Thanks for your friendship. I don't know what I'd do without it."

"We all need each other, don't we?"

Kay waved her hand, opened the car door and put up the umbrella.

"Don't get too wet," Roberta called as Kay ran to her house. She watched Kay duck through the doorway. She started the car and headed home. On the way she felt a lump in her throat. A simple prayer flitted through her mind. *Thank you, Lord, that I have my dear husband there for me at home.*

Tessa knocked on the door and pushed it open. "Sherry?" she called softly as she entered the room. She almost gasped. Sherry, pale and still swathed in bandages, looked nothing like the healthy, vibrant friend she had last seen in Angel Fire.

Sherry's eyes flew open. "Tessa! Oh, I'm so glad to see you," she exclaimed. "I'm going crazy lying in this bed all day."

Tessa came to the bed and handed Sherry the card and set a vase of flowers down on the bedside table. "These are from our breakfast group," she said. "Everyone is so sorry about the accident."

Sherry opened the card and quickly read the words. "Please tell them all thank you. I wish I was in Taos so I might get some more company. At least some friends have called."

Tessa pulled the one chair closer to the bed and sat down. "Do you know how long you'll be here?" she asked.

"Well, I've started on rehab already, and they've said I will be moved to the rehab facility soon. I'll be there a couple of weeks, then I can go home and continue doing the therapy up there."

"Oh," Tessa added, trying to lighten the mood. "You mean Bob's House of Horrors," she joked. "Bob's really good And there's a new young man there now, Greg. He's also good."

Sherry seemed to brighten up at this fresh bit of information. "Catch me up on all the news from Angel Fire," Sherry asked, an eager edge to her voice.

The two talked for a while, the subjects ranging from who'd been to Zeb's, all the bear reports, the upcoming Balloon Festival, even the weather. While they had been talking about Angel Fire things Sherry began to show a little of her usual sparkle. Sherry was one of those people always ready with a smile, someone with a zest for life. The person Tessa saw in front of her had a long way to go to get back to being that familiar, enthusiastic person. She began to wonder how she could possibly bring up a question about the pills. It was obvious that Sherry didn't want to talk about the accident at all. Tessa slipped her hand into her pocket, putting her fingers around the small zip-lock bag she had put the pills in.

An orderly bustled into the room. "Time for your therapy. Sorry to break up your visit." The young man pulled the waiting wheelchair toward the bed.

I'll wait till next time to ask about the pills, Tessa thought, and was a little surprised at her sense of relief. *I'm sure there's a logical explanation.* The two said their goodbyes and Tessa promised to come again when she could.

When Tessa got back in the car with Jim her thoughts remained with Sherry, her situation, and the pills. *I know Ed was quite a ladies' man. Maybe they were his pills, and they were . . .* "Jim," she said suddenly, "what does Viagra look like?

"What?" exclaimed her husband. "What brought that on?"

"Oh, nothing, really. Just wondering."

"As your husband, I think I should know why you're wondering about Viagra." Jim glanced at her as he turned out of the parking lot. His expression was between confusion and amusement.

"Uh, it was a joke Sherry was telling me about Viagra. So, what does it look like?"

"It's a little blue pill, and one I hope you don't think I need."

"Oh, no. No, it's nothing like that. I was curious, that's all."

"So, what was the joke?"

"The joke?"

"Yeah, the joke about Viagra."

"Jim, you know I never remember the punch line of jokes." She paused, glancing out the window. "So, are we going to Costco now?"

The Saturday of the Balloon Festival dawned as a picture-perfect day, just as expected. Pick-ups, SUVs, and cars lined up along route 434 near the airport well ahead of the opening time for the mass ascension. The buzz of excitement filled the air as balloons of every color were unfurled. Everywhere young children fairly bounced with excitement, teens nudged each other and pointed, and adults smiled as they wandered around breathing in the mountain air and the unique atmosphere of this colorful, early dawn experience.

Roberta, Kay, and Al made their way through the crowd, admiring the patterns and hues. They paused here and there talking with friends, watching the one balloon that was tethered nearby giving opportunities for a ride.

"Do you ladies want to go up?" asked Al. "I'll be glad to stay down here and watch you."

They both shook their heads firmly. "No, thanks," said Roberta. "I like old terra firma."

The sizzle of tension mounted as the flames burst into the air, the balloons growing larger and larger, lifting to the sky. At that magical moment when they launched the baskets upward, when the vibrant hues of the balloons filled the sky, a universal gasp of awe came from the watching crowd. The balloons went higher and higher, and everyone on the ground was craning their necks to keep them in view. Those who were manning the chase vehicles ran to their trucks and started off, ready to follow the balloons to their point of landing.

Suddenly, one of the drivers began running back across the field, yelling something to the balloon pilot way above him. Roberta, Kay, and Al could barely make out his words, but he was definitely yelling, "You've got the keys!" The balloons were too high for his voice to reach them.

"Oh, my gosh," said Al. "What is he going to do?"

Before anyone could answer, another man with a pick-up truck yelled, "Come on! We can use my truck!" and the two men jumped in a red pick-up and careened their way out of the airport.

"That could have been a real problem," said Roberta, shaking her head.

Kay nodded. "For sure." She smiled at Roberta and Al. "Thanks for bringing me here today. I enjoyed it."

Roberta put her arm around her friend's shoulders as they walked back to their car. The sun climbed higher, the balloons glided their way across the sky, and Roberta declared it a good morning.

6

After Jim's final putt on the last hole, Tessa, Jim, Roberta and Al walked back to the golf carts and climbed in. It had been a perfect morning for golf, the temperature in the low 70s, not a cloud in the sky, and the beauty of the mountains around them. Al was still annoyed about the ball that had bounced its way into the rushing creek (though Al didn't think it was even an official creek), and he continued to complain to Jim.

"It may not be a creek," Jim said, "but it's taken your ball and fled. Sorry."

"You don't have to gloat about it," mumbled Al under his breath.

The puttering of the golf cart's motor silenced the conversation as they wound their way back toward the club house

With the morning of golf behind them, the two couples found an outside table after placing their lunch order at the grill. The men continued their bantering about golf strokes and scores, and Roberta turned to Tessa and asked about her visit with Sherry.

Tessa frowned. "Well, she seemed to be doing as well as possible. Her leg is in a cast, and her arm is heavily bandaged. Her face still has the cuts and bruises, and lots of gauze bandages around her head. Her morale is pretty good considering everything."

"What did she say about the accident?"

"Nothing, really. We didn't talk about the accident at all. I told her we were all sorry about it, and she didn't respond. I didn't think I should bring it up, or talk about Ed or anything. Really, Bertie, I didn't know if I should say any more or not."

Roberta nodded. "Mmm. It's hard to know what to do in those circumstances, with Ed being killed. I can't imagine how she feels."

"I can't either. We didn't even mention Ed's name." Tessa thought about those white pills suddenly. *Should I mention them to Bertie? What if she tells me to turn them in to the police? Am I ready to do that without giving Sherry a chance to explain herself?*

Their food arrived and the talk shifted to general topics, especially the condition of the roads.

"There's going to be a bad accident soon with drivers swerving all over to miss the giant pot holes," said Al.

"At least we don't need to budget for speed bumps," Roberta commented. "We can't go fast while trying to avoid potholes."

Tessa set down her iced tea. "Except, some people still do. Something needs to be done."

"But what? It would cost millions to fix the roads. The village doesn't have that kind of money."

"If they'd bite the bullet and fix them properly instead of merely doing a Band-Aid fix over and over, it would be better. They'll end up spending as much money on these temporary fixes as they would if they simply did it right the first time," Al said.

The four turned to their lunch, knowing that this was a problem without a solution at this time.

On Tuesday, amid the babble of breakfast noises and aromas of coffee and bacon, Olivia looked around the breakfast group. "Have any of you heard from Wanda? I saw a light on in her house again last night."

No one had any recent news about their friend. "I had an email about two weeks ago," said Annabelle. "She said they would be late getting here this year because of some project of her husband's. I don't expect her for another couple of weeks."

"Well, there was definitely a light in their house. I'm sure of it this time."

"Maybe someone from the property management company was checking on the house."

"At night? I doubt it," said Olivia.

"Well, maybe they left a light on by mistake," suggested Annabelle. "That real estate company Sherry works for does their property management, I know. Maybe you should call and mention that you saw a light left on."

"Was there a car in the driveway?" asked Myra.

Olivia shook her head. "It might have been in the garage. The garage door was closed, so I don't know."

Roberta smiled. "Believe me, even if they got in late last night, Wanda would be here this morning. She'd never miss a Tuesday morning breakfast."

The group chuckled. "None of us would," said Tessa.

Annabelle added, "How would we know anything about what was going on in Angel Fire?"

"Which reminds me," began Myra, leaning forward. "I've heard that Ed's children—he had a grown son and daughter, I think—are going to sue Sherry."

"Sue Sherry! Why?" exclaimed Tessa.

"They say she must have been the driver. They said Ed was such an experienced driver that even if he had to swerve, he wouldn't have lost control."

"That's ridiculous," said Roberta. "Anyone could have lost control."

"Besides, how could they prove who was driving?" asked Tessa. "They were both thrown from the jeep."

Myra nodded. "Only one way. Someone had to see them in the car as they went up the mountain. There has to be a witness about who was actually driving."

"What will happen if Sherry was driving?" Tessa asked, a worried frown on her face.

"Well," said Myra, "it will be terrible for her. I think the family is talking of taking her to civil court so it would simply be a financial loss.

You know Sherry, as a single parent she has struggled so hard financially over the years and she could lose everything. At her age, she could never catch up again. It would be disastrous."

"If they won in civil court, do you think some criminal charges might follow?" asked Annabelle.

"No doubt." Myra said.

The group remained quiet for a moment, absorbing the somber repercussions for Sherry of the terrible accident.

"Let's change the subject and talk about something pleasant," said Kay, who had remained silent throughout. "Has anyone found anything exceptionally good at the farmers' market lately?"

That's all it took for the conversations to take off in several different directions about produce and recipes. Roberta and Tessa exchanged a look that spoke volumes about their mutual concern for Sherry.

"Annabelle, that's such a pretty outfit you have on today. Are you headed to Taos or Santa Fe or somewhere?" asked Olivia.

"No, I'll be here in Angel Fire all day."

"Annabelle always looks like she's dressed up for something," Myra said.

"Well, I think it's important to always look your best. It makes a person feel better when they're dressed nicely. Besides, don't forget that I'm from that generation that dressed up for everything. When we'd travel by train or plane, we'd wear our Sunday best, high heels, gloves, even hats."

"I remember dressing that way for church," said Roberta. "I'd never go to church without a hat."

"And remember girdles?" asked Myra, chuckling.

Tessa and Olivia looked from one to another.

"Of course, you young things wouldn't even know about that. We had these awful things, some were even made out of rubber, or something like that. We'd pull and yank and try to pour our bodies into them, kind of like stuffed sausages."

"And stockings!" added Annabelle. "Remember when they had seams, and you were always trying to keep them straight."

"I've seen pictures of them," said Tessa. "I can't imagine wearing them."

"And we never wore jeans, or slacks to school, even in the winter. When it was really bitter cold, we could wear slacks under our dresses, but we had to take them off when we got to school. Crazy!" Myra said.

"During the war—that's World War II, girls—my mother worked at a man's job. She needed to wear pants. Of course, there was no such thing easily available for women, so she had to make her own."

Olivia shook her head. "Things have really changed between that generation and ours. I like our way a lot better."

"I'm not sure I do," said Roberta. "I liked wearing hats and gloves for special occasions."

Olivia made a face. "What about girdles?"

Everyone laughed, and agreed that it was good they were a thing of the past.

Kay stayed quiet during the drive back to her house from breakfast. Roberta glanced at her a time or two, wondering if Myra's reference to the accident had put Kay back in her deep grief again. Roberta braked carefully when three doe and a fawn skittered their way across the road in front of them.

As they stopped in her driveway, Kay said, "I won't be going to breakfast next week, Bertie, so you won't need to pick me up."

"Not going? Why? Was it because of Myra's comments?"

Kay shook her head. "No, nothing like that. Heather, Dick and the boys will be here next week, that's all."

"Oh, that'll be nice," Roberta said with obvious relief. "Why don't you and Heather come to breakfast? Everyone will be glad to see her. It's been a while."

"We'll see," said Kay. "I like to have time alone with them while they're here."

"I understand. Think about it, though. I'd love to see her again."

"Maybe we can have lunch together, or something," Kay commented over her shoulder as she got out of the car. "I'll call you."

"OK," Roberta replied. "Have fun." She backed the car out of the driveway as Kay went into her house.

Olivia wound her way home on Via del Rey after dropping Tessa back home. She noticed the wildflowers in bloom along the way, the purple iris and the white yarrow with their feathery leaves. As she passed Wanda's house, she slowed her Bronco. She saw no signs of life at the house, so she continued on her way. At the next cul de sac, however, she swung into it, turned the Bronco around, and headed back. She pulled into the Smith's driveway, cut off the motor, and sat staring at the house. *There's no light now in that room now. Why do I feel uneasy about this?* she wondered.

After a moment or two, she got out of the Bronco and went to the door, knocking loudly. The sound reverberated through the quiet of the morning. She waited, then knocked again. There was not a sound from the house, its stucco walls holding in the apparent emptiness.

Olivia looked around, and then walked to the back of the house. The silence of the mountain morning followed her. She saw that there were no bird feeders out, the plastic hummingbird container was empty, and the planters on the deck had no flowers in them. Wanda was definitely not there yet.

As Olivia continued her way around the other side of the house, something out of place caught in her peripheral vision, something blue and yellow. She walked closer and was surprised to see a blue towel spread over the deck railing. She walked slowly to it, put her hand on the towel and gasped.

The blue towel with a bright yellow sun in the middle was wet.

7

Olivia's glance went to the sliding doors of the deck, fully expecting someone to be there staring at her. With relief, she saw no one. She hurried to her car, her gaze sweeping around. Once inside the Bronco, she slammed the door shut. *This is creepy. Something is going on, but what?* With a final glance around, Olivia started the vehicle and left.

Back home, Olivia wandered around her house restlessly. She walked into the studio and walked up to the easel. She didn't feel like working on her latest painting, a stand of aspen dressed in their golden foliage with the sun shining through. Much as she loved working with the light and shadow in the painting, she couldn't get up any enthusiasm for it today. She rubbed her arms as if chilled, even though she didn't really feel cold.

She sat at her desk and opened her computer. It seemed to take forever to boot up, as usual, but finally she was able to click on her email. No interesting emails from anyone. There was a coupon offer from Target. She'd let that go since there wasn't a Target anywhere near Angel Fire. She clicked on "Compose" and entered Wanda's email address. *I don't want her to worry about their house, though. I'll only ask when they're going to arrive. Should I ask if they're letting anyone use their house? No, that might make her suspicious. They've never had anyone use their house before. I'll wait and see what she says.*

After writing the email Olivia hit "Send" and felt a little better. If Sherry had been at the real estate office that took care of the Smith's house, Olivia wouldn't hesitate to call and ask about the light. *Maybe I'll call tomorrow anyway. I'll see how I feel in the morning. I don't want to seem like a busybody sticking my nose in something that's none of my business.* She straightened her shoulders, took a deep breath, and decided to work in her studio after all.

Olivia entered the bright room and, as usual, she felt a shift in her mood. The whole ambiance of the studio uplifted her, the smell of turpentine and paint, the light, airy feel of the room, the view of the mountains through the huge windows. She looked around at the number of canvasses stacked against the walls.

Maybe it's time to organize these and get some to the galleries, she thought. Only last week she'd had a call from her favorite gallery in Taos asking for more paintings with the Spanish churches in them. She'd completed several of those a few months ago.

Olivia began going through her completed work, sorting them in her somewhat haphazard method according to topics. After rearranging them all, she looked around with a puzzled expression. *I know I had several more with Spanish churches. Did I already take them to one of the galleries? Maybe they sold at the last show I went to in Albuquerque and I forgot to make a note of it. Am I losing my mind? I'm not that old, but they say this is what happens when you get older, and it's happening to Mom already. Is it happening to me, too?*

"The traffic up here is getting so bad," exclaimed Annabelle at the next Tuesday breakfast gathering. "This morning at the stop sign I had to wait for three cars in each direction before I could pull out on Route 434."

Tessa laughed. "Why, we might even need a traffic light here someday."

"It's the summer people," Myra explained, as if they didn't all know how popular the cool mountain air of an Angel Fire summer was, especially for people coming from the heat and humidity of Texas and Oklahoma.

"Well, our economy needs these seasonal people. After all, we have a top-rate golf course in the summer and a great ski mountain in the winter."

"Not to mention a world class chamber music festival. It should be really special this year since it's Ida Kavafian's thirtieth year as Music Director."

"You all sound like the Chamber of Commerce," chided Annabelle. "And watch what you say. Remember, I'm a summer person too."

"Personally, I'm always glad to see the summer people. It's like old friends week when Evelyn Bochow, J.Sue Topping, and people like that get here," said Roberta, and everyone nodded. "And this summer, Pat Pangrac's daughter, Sherry Vacik, will be coming all the way from Prague."

"By the way," began Olivia. She'd been sitting quietly, thinking how to bring the subject up. "I went by Wanda's house last Tuesday on my way home. I actually parked and knocked, but there was no answer. I walked around the house. It was obvious they weren't here yet. I noticed a towel hanging on the deck railing. And it was wet."

Roberta shrugged. "That could have been from the house cleaners or something."

Olivia raised her eyebrows. "It could have been but when I went by the next day, checking again, it was gone. I emailed Wanda to see when they would be coming, and she said they would get here next Monday."

"Do you think they're delayed because of their grandson, Mason?" Annabelle looked from one to another.

"Is he the one who's autistic?" asked Tessa.

Roberta nodded. "He's about eight-years-old now. They had taken him to a new doctor last year, I believe, and the doctor had a number of good recommendations about things that might be helpful for Mason"

"You hear so much about autism these days," said Annabelle. "Do you think it's more common, or has it always been there and is now more easily diagnosed?"

Tessa shrugged.

Myra spoke up. "I read an article about it recently. The statistics say it actually is becoming more common. Some researchers think it's because of toxic things in our environment, like pesticides."

"That's what I've been telling you all!" put in Tessa, leaning forward. "We have to become smarter about all those things we're putting in our food."

"Oh, Lordy, what have I started?" said Myra, rolling her eyes. "Tessa, we don't need one of your lectures. We believe you. Let's get back to Wanda. Does anyone know why they're delayed this year?"

"I think it's because of something Robert's doing."

"But what about their house? What do you think is happening there?" asked Tessa.

"I don't know. Maybe nothing. It gives me a weird feeling, though, but I couldn't say why."

Roberta looked around at the group. "Do you think we ought to notify the police?"

"It's not really any of our business," said Annabelle.

Myra gave Annabelle one of her withering glances. "Anything that happens in Angel Fire is our business. We're a small community, and we need to look out for each other."

The group had trouble repressing smiles knowing that Myra really did consider anyone's business her business.

Olivia shrugged. "I guess we should wait and see. I drive by there all the time and I can keep an eye on the house."

"Since Kay's not here this week we can talk about Ed and Sherry's accident," said Tessa. "Has anyone heard any more about whether or not Sherry will be sued?"

"Oh, there could definitely be a case filed in civil court," said Myra. "It will be a shame for Sherry if they find out that she was the driver."

The group murmured their agreement. "Why are his kids suing?" asked Tessa.

"Who knows? I wouldn't be surprised if some ambulance-chasing kind of lawyer went to them and said he could get them a better inheritance by suing, and then they would get all that money in addition to whatever they would have inherited."

"That's ridiculous. Sherry doesn't have any money."

"Well, Ed's kids don't know that. Anyway, there's probably more to it than money." Myra wore the look of someone in the know, as she so often did. "I've heard that after their mother's death, the kids wanted Ed to move closer to them. Instead he took off for this 'wilderness' place known as Angel Fire. Not only that, then he started going out with women. I guess they worried that he'd up and marry someone, and there might go all their inheritance."

Annabelle sighed. "I never wanted to tell Kay this, but I saw Ed with lots of different women even when they were seeing so much of each other."

Looking at her watch and feeling a need to end the speculation and gossip, Roberta said, "I'm taking a load to Angel's Attic today. Does anyone have anything they want me to take?" Angel's Attic was the thrift shop in Eagle Nest run by the Baptist Church to make clothing and household items available to those who might be struggling financially, as many were in northern New Mexico. No one had anything to contribute, so Roberta stood, gathered her purse and keys, and the friends bid their goodbyes, also rising, and heading their separate ways.

Roberta turned right at the blinking light and headed toward Eagle Nest. She never passed the entrance to the Vietnam Veterans' Memorial that she didn't think of the impressive "Run for the Wall" that happened every May. Hundreds and hundreds of bikers came roaring through the area on their way to the Memorial Wall in Washington D.C. The community provided their dinner and breakfast the next morning.

She thought about the time she and Al had spent a week in the nation's capital, simply being tourists and taking in all the memorials and the numerous Smithsonian museums. The cherry blossoms had burst into bloom around the basin and the Jefferson Memorial. She had thought it was one of the most beautiful sights to see. They had continued on the trolley ride, getting on and off as they chose to see the various places. At the Lincoln Memorial they got off the ride and climbed the steps for that impressive view, then walked down to the beginning of the black wall of the Vietnam Memorial that carried the names of the over 58,000 lost during that tragic time in the nation's history. She and Al had searched for the names of those from Al's hometown who had been killed. When they located them, Al had taken paper and pencil and rubbed over the carving, copying the names onto the paper. As Roberta waited for him, she had watched the visitors to the wall; men in combat fatigues, their faces lined, their eyes downcast, their pain almost palpable; parents with children who left cards in childish scrawl saying "Dear Grandpa"; others touching the names, tears slipping from their eyes. Roberta had felt that she was in a sacred place.

Now, passing by Angel Fire's Memorial to the veterans of that time, Roberta cleared her throat to remove the lump that had formed. She had seen the same kinds of expressions on those who visited this memorial, and she was so glad they had such a place here in the mountains. The chapel of the Memorial was open 24/7, and the view out over the peaceful valley could help those visiting find some sense of comfort. She made her way on toward Eagle Nest, putting those feelings aside as the miles passed and enjoying the drive as she always did, with the mountains around her.

Sherry hung up the phone by her hospital bed at the rehab facility with a sigh. So many details to take care of, and she had such limited energy. *At least Amber can be here for a week when I make the adjustment back to Angel Fire.* Sherry had returned from her therapy session when her landlord had called wondering about her plans. She was extremely anxious to return to work as soon as possible, in fact, it was imperative. Her meager savings would not last long if she was not working.

Sherry looked up as the door to her room opened. "Tessa! I'm so glad to see you," she exclaimed.

"We had more errands in Albuquerque so I hoped to get by before we had to head back. You know the routine; doctor's appointment, Costco, and Sam's."

"Oh, yes. Well, I'll be getting back to Angel Fire soon myself, and I can hardly wait."

"That's great." Tessa smiled at her friend. "So, what's the plan?"

"They told me this morning, I'll be released from this rehab place next week. Amber is coming out to drive me back to Angel Fire, and she'll stay a week to help me settle in."

"I guess you'll be able to continue your therapy up there?"

Sherry nodded enthusiastically. "Having that physical therapy facility in Angel Fire is a real blessing. Hopefully, I can work my therapy sessions around my working hours."

"You're planning on going back to work soon?" asked Tessa.

"I have to. I can't afford not to have the income. Fortunately, it's my left leg that was broken, so I should be able to drive soon. My arm cast comes off before I get released."

Tessa fingered the little bag with the mysterious white pills that she'd slipped into her pocket, but she still hesitated to mention them.

Sherry leaned back onto her pillows and sighed. "This has been such an ordeal, Tessa. I can't get over how much a person's life can change in the blink of an eye." A tear slowly slid from the corner of her eye.

Tessa leaned forward and laid her hand gently on Sherry's arm. "We all hate that this has happened to you. You know you have a lot of friends up in Angel Fire who will be there to help you when you get home."

Sherry wiped away her tear brusquely. "I know. And, believe me, I'll really be appreciating them. It's so awful when I let myself think of what happened. About Ed and all. I still can't believe it."

"Maybe it's just as well that you don't remember the accident," Tessa said.

"Yes and no. I can't stand thinking that I *was* possibly the driver. Maybe I'll remember as time goes on. I have had a couple of flashes of memory. The other day, out of the blue, I remembered that we had lunch at Doc Martin's. Although then, I couldn't remember what I had ordered or anything else. It's so weird."

Since Sherry had brought up that day, Tessa took a deep breath and pulled the pills out of her pocket. "Do you know anything about these?" she asked, holding them out to Sherry. "I found them near the accident site when Jim and I were hiking."

Sherry reached for the packet of pills with shaking hands.

Her eyes had an expression full of alarm.

8

There was an electric silence in the room as Tessa waited for a response from Sherry. Sherry's gaze never left the white pills clutched in her hand.

"I know what kind of pills these are," Sherry admitted in a shaky voice. "They've given them to me in the hospital. They're oxycodone. They're a narcotic. An extremely strong narcotic."

"Do you know anything about them?"

"I know they're often sold on the street."

The two sat silently for the thumping of a heartbeat. Sherry handed the package back to Tessa. "You'd better get rid of these. If you're caught with them, you could be charged with illegal possession or something."

Tessa gulped. "I never thought of that! I'll get rid of them, but, Sherry, were they yours or Ed's? I found them there at the accident site."

Sherry drew her hand back quickly. "No! Neither Ed nor I had anything to do with them, or with any drugs. At least, I don't think Ed did, and I *know* I didn't. What are you going to do about them?"

"I needed to be sure they weren't yours or Ed's," Tessa said. "I haven't known what to do with them, whether I should give them to the police or what."

"Did you show them to anyone else?" asked Sherry.

"I didn't dare, until I talked to you. I almost asked Roberta once, and then decided not to mention the pills to anyone, not even Jim." Tessa rose and walked to the bathroom, opened the zip-lock bag and dumped the pills in the toilet. After being sure they all flushed away, she went back and sat by Sherry's bed. "Well, that's taken care of," she said firmly."

"Tessa, honestly, those pills weren't mine. You do believe me, don't you?"

"Yes, I believe you," Tessa hesitated a brief second. "The question still is 'What were they doing at the accident scene?'"

"I have no idea. I do know that I don't take drugs. Please believe me. And I can't imagine that Ed would take them either."

Tessa sat silently for a moment. "But you don't remember anything about that day, do you?"

"Tessa!"

"I'm not implying anything, Sherry. I only want to be sure. Anyway, the pills are gone now so there isn't an issue anymore. Let's put that behind us."

"Oh, God, how I'd like to put the whole thing behind me! I wish . . . " Tears began flowing from Sherry's eyes. "There are so many things I wish had never happened. Those few seconds and now my life has changed forever."

Tessa put her hand on Sherry's arm. "I know. I'm sorry I brought up something so upsetting, but I had to know. I believe you about the pills, Sherry. We won't ever talk about them again." She handed Sherry some tissues from the box on her nightstand, and the two friends visited for a few more minutes before Tessa left to meet her husband.

After Tessa left, Sherry leaned back onto the pillows, staring ahead and biting her lower lip. *What really happened that day? Why can't I remember? Did Ed actually have something to do with those pills?*

Roberta sat on the deck with Al in that comfortable time after the dinner dishes are done and before the light fades from the sky. They watched a small buck make his way through the greenbelt behind their yard. A dog barked in the distance. The buck's head jerked up and he stood poised and still. Assured there was no danger, he continued grazing, and then silently slipped away into the gathering dusk.

"A penny for your thoughts," Al said. He had observed that his wife had been quieter than usual throughout dinner.

Roberta sighed and set down her wine glass. "I can't get Kay and Ed and Sherry, and all that situation, off my mind. We were talking about it at breakfast, and Annabelle said she had actually seen Ed with a lot of other women, even while he and Kay were going together."

Al gave a little snort. "Ed would hardly have said he and Kay were 'going together'. I played golf with him, remember? He was always bragging about some conquest, some woman who was interested in him. He was quite the ladies' man, believe me."

Roberta sat up straighter, an indignant look on her face. "Al Streit, why didn't you tell me? I could have warned Kay what kind of man he was. She could have been spared a lot of heartbreak."

Al gave his wife a puzzled look. "It wasn't any of my business what Ed did. Guys don't come home and tell their wives all the b.s. conversation that goes on at the golf course. All Kay had to do was look around and she would have seen Ed with other women. He certainly never made a secret of it."

"Well, I wasn't aware of it or I would have warned her. Anyway, it doesn't matter now, does it? I feel sorry for all of them. Ed's family is suing Sherry, you know, saying she was the driver."

"Don't see how they can say who the driver was."

Roberta nodded. "Exactly. Sherry doesn't remember anything about the accident."

"Yeah, and that's pretty convenient, isn't it?"

"Al! You know Sherry. How could you think she's lying about that?"

"I didn't say she was lying. I simply observed that it was convenient, that's all."

"How do you think it will be resolved, the case I mean?" Roberta looked at her husband as she waited for his answer. She knew he would consider all the factors in a reasonable way, and she also knew he had good instincts about such things. She had relied on his level-headed understanding of things for all their years together.

He shrugged. "Can't say for sure. I can't believe anything will come of it. I don't see how they could ever determine who was driving unless some witness comes forward. I think it will be OK for Sherry."

"I hope so," said Roberta, gazing into the distance as the last light faded from the sky. "I really hope so."

"Wanda! You're back!" exclaimed Annabelle as Wanda Smith entered the coffee shop on Tuesday morning.

"Finally," Wanda said with a smile as she went around the table giving everyone a hug. She was dressed as usual in jeans and a tee shirt that proclaimed a message. This one said "I'm not short, I'm fun size." She squeezed her 5'1", busty body onto a chair, leaned forward and said, "So, tell me everything that's been going on."

As usual, everyone began talking at once. Wanda laughed her throaty laugh, tossed her curly, blonde head, and held up her hands. "Whoa," she said. "One at a time."

Myra began. "Well, the biggest news is the big accident last month. Up on the pass. Ed Wilson and Sherry Sullivan were on their way home from Taos in his jeep." The friends all seemed to be making a deliberate effort not to look at Kay. Wanda's surprise prevented her from doing the same.

"Ed and Sherry?" she exclaimed.

Kay kept her gaze lowered, picked up her coffee cup and took a sip as Myra continued.

"They were both thrown from the jeep. Ed was killed and Sherry was seriously injured."

"Killed?" Wanda couldn't help but glance at Kay again. "That's terrible!"

Roberta continued the story. "Sherry was airlifted to Albuquerque. She is coming back to Angel Fire this week, though, with her daughter."

"I'll be taking them a casserole," put in Myra quickly.

Wanda smiled. "Of course."

"When did you get in?" asked Annabelle.

"Yesterday afternoon. I hated that we were late getting here this year. You know Robert. He got involved in a project at church and wanted to finish up before we left."

"How was everything at your house?" asked Olivia.

"Fine," said Wanda. "It always feels so good to get back."

"Was anyone staying at your house before you came?" Olivia couldn't resist asking.

"No. Why did you ask that?" Wanda looked at Olivia with a puzzled expression on her face.

Olivia shrugged. "Just wondering. I thought I'd seen a light on one time. Maybe it was cleaning people or something."

"No, we don't have any cleaning done before we come."

"Oh." She paused. "Then I saw a blue towel with a big sunburst in the center hanging on the deck railing."

"A blue towel with a sunburst? We don't have any towels like that up here. Are you sure?"

Olivia nodded. "A blue towel with a bright yellow sun in the center."

Wanda sat back and frowned. "That is odd and creepy. Everything was exactly as we left it, though."

"I'm sure there's some logical explanation," said Roberta. "Tell us about your winter. How are all the grandkids?"

"They're all doing well, thanks. Mason started doing equine therapy this year, and it has really helped him. He loves it.

"What is equine therapy?" asked Annabelle.

"It's really just horseback riding. They have people leading the horses around the ring. Evidently, something about the feel of the horse or relating with the horse, or something, is good for children who are autistic. They build an emotional connection with the horse which often helps them come out of their shell. It's quite amazing to see. It's hard for Mason to talk to people yet he talks to the horse and has this huge smile the whole time he's riding. Being around the horses seems to calm him in some way and it also seems to be helping him with his communication skills in daily life. We are so excited that he has an activity like this to look forward to each week."

"That's wonderful," said Olivia.

"You know, there's such a range of autism, and, fortunately, Mason's isn't extreme. He can function on a pretty high level compared to a lot of children. Here, let me show you some photos." Wanda pulled out her iPhone with the latest pictures, and conversations took off again.

Sherry hobbled on her crutches through the office door of the real estate company as her daughter held it open for her. She made her way to her desk and plopped into her swivel chair. She stretched her leg with the brace and boot until it could be situated comfortably—or as comfortably as possible—under the desk. Her daughter took the crutches from her and leaned them against the wall within reach.

"Whew!" Sherry exclaimed. "I didn't think that would take so much energy."

Amber smiled at her mom. "Hopefully, it will get easier each day. I'm sorry I can only stay a week to help you, Mom." Amber was the image of her mother, tall, blonde, with blue eyes. After graduating from Cimarron High School and the University of New Mexico, she had taken a job with Delta in Atlanta. Sherry hated that she was so far away, but Amber could fly free so they could work in visits fairly often. Sherry wondered what would happen, though, when Amber married and had a family. *Will I want to leave Angel Fire then in order to be near Amber and her family?,* Sherry often wondered, although she couldn't imagine ever wanting to leave Angel Fire.

"I'm sure in a week I'll be getting around by myself. Thanks for getting me here today. Now, you can go on and do whatever you want to, and I'll spend the day trying to catch up. I've got my cell phone if I need you. I'll be fine, and you can plan on picking me up around four this afternoon." Sherry was already sifting through all the messages on her desk. There were file folders stacked high on one corner, and a pile of blue 'You have a message' notes in the center. She barely noticed when Amber waved good bye and headed out the door.

Moments later Hannah Meyrick opened the door and stopped short when she saw Sherry.

Oh, I . . . I didn't know you were back."

Sherry looked up at the young woman. "Hi, Hannah. Yes, finally I'm back. How is everything going? Have you been getting all the cleaning assignments since I wasn't here?'

"Yeah, sure. Everyone has filtered them down to me directly. It's worked out OK."

"Good. How's Shandra doing? Are you all managing?"

"It isn't easy, but we're making it." Hannah stood looking around uneasily.

"Did you want to see me about something, Hannah? I haven't had time to catch up on what houses need to be cleaned yet. I can let you know this afternoon."

"Oh, no, that's OK. I only needed to return a key."

Sherry pulled open the middle drawer and removed a key, unlocking the side drawer where the keys were kept. She kept reading the pile of notes on her desk and Hannah came forward and placed a key quickly in its place in the drawer. Hannah scurried back to the door and called good bye as she was leaving.

"Whose house were you cleaning?" asked Sherry.

"One of the usual, the Williams' house," she said, and she slipped through the doorway, quickly closing the door behind.

Sherry went back to her papers, trying to get a sense of which of the houses she managed needed attention.

9

Roberta rested an extra moment on her exercise mat at the Community Center before getting up. *Does the fact that these exercises seem harder mean that I'm getting older?* She wondered.

"Need a hand up?" Olivia asked, smiling as she extended her hand.

Roberta's laugh had a rueful edge to it. "No, thanks. I just need an extra minute—or a younger body." She pushed herself up and began rolling up her mat.

"I understand," said Olivia. "What I miss most is my mind."

"Oh, I have that problem, too." The two friends made their way out of the gym where their exercise class had been meeting for years.

"Seriously," Olivia began, a worried look on her face, "Last week I really did wonder about my mind. I know I had painted some more of my Spanish church scenes, but when I started looking for them, I couldn't find them. They simply are not in my studio. I couldn't remember if I'd sold them at my last show, or what."

"I wish I could say you'd given them to me. I love your landscapes with the Spanish churches."

"Thanks. Bertie, have you noticed any changes in me lately? Am I getting more forgetful or anything?" Olivia paused as Roberta began to open her car door.

Roberta gave her an encouraging smile. "Olivia, my dear friend, you have been forgetful for as long as I've known you. I've always attributed it to your creative nature."

"But have you noticed any difference?"

"No, there isn't any difference. Now, stop worrying and go home and paint some more."

Olivia's tense expression finally relaxed. "OK. That's a great idea. It's only that . . . well, you know, my mom is beginning to show signs of dementia. And she's so young to be doing that. I was afraid that maybe it runs in the family. Maybe I was already having those problems."

Roberta looked at Olivia and realized that she was seriously worried. "Olivia, you do not show any signs of dementia, I promise you. You've never paid attention to the business side of your painting. That's the only problem, I'm sure. Are you worried about your mom? Have things gotten worse?"

"I think my dad tries to keep us from knowing that mom isn't doing as well. When I called last week, well, mom answered and said in a real nervous voice 'Who is this?', and I said, 'It's Olivia, Mom.' She said 'Who?' and I said, 'Mom, it's Olivia, your daughter', and she said 'Olivia?' like she didn't know who that was. Then I heard some muffled conversation and Dad came on the phone. He said he'd been putting away the breakfast dishes. I asked what was wrong with mom, and he said she was having a bad day. He told me not to worry, that she'd be OK. The last time I'd visited, about two weeks ago, she was fine. She knew who I was and we had a good time together. Now, though, I don't know what to think." Olivia looked away as if studying the distant mountains while she tried to get her emotions under control.

"I know it must be so hard to see this happening," Roberta said.

Olivia could only nod.

"I can assure you, you are fine, Olivia. I'm so sorry you are having to deal with this with your mom. Don't take on any added burden by thinking you have dementia because you don't."

Olivia gave a weak smile. "OK. Thanks."

"So, can you go and lose yourself in painting for the rest of the day?"

"I hope so."

Roberta patted Olivia's arm. "Good. See you later."

Roberta backed her car out of the parking place and headed back down toward Route 434, the main street through Angel Fire. As she passed the life-size elk statue in the median strip she waved at Margie Evans and some of the garden club members working on the plantings there and admired the beautiful flowers. Her thoughts, though, were on Olivia's words, wondering if, in fact, there was some subtle difference in her friend's behavior. Although everyone agreed that Olivia was a little on the scatter-brained side, it wasn't like her to misplace several of her paintings.

This growing older is definitely not for sissies, Roberta mused. Why had her mother never told her about all the concerns, the aches and pains, the fears of what the future might hold? Come to think about it, why had her mother never told her about *anything*? That was such a different generation, a different time. Her parents' generation never spoke openly about feelings, never mentioned anything that might remotely have to do with sex. Children were to be seen and not heard. The fathers were the breadwinners and the moms all stayed at home. Quite a change from today.

Her thoughts turned to a conversation among the Tuesday morning group one time, comparing their different backgrounds and upbringings. That was when she first realized that she was probably the oldest of the group, except for Annabelle, and that there were some basic differences in the way she looked at life and the way those more than ten years younger, like Tessa did.

"Well, anyway," she muttered out loud, straightening her shoulders, "age is only a number that doesn't really mean anything anymore."

After finishing her yogurt and granola bar for lunch, Sherry pushed back her chair and stretched her arms overhead. She had been bent over her desk, computer and phone all morning and the crick in her neck was getting worse. Somehow, lying in bed for the day no longer seemed an unbearably boring way to spend time, as it had been such a short time ago.

She pulled her calendar closer to enter in the notations on the various rental properties which she managed. She flipped the pages back to double check something when her glance caught a notation that made her heart feel like it had skipped a beat. It was a brief note in her handwriting for a Saturday last month: *Taos with Ed. Discuss Denver?*

Sherry's eyes filled with tears and her lower lip trembled. She had tried so hard not to think about that day, about the unspeakable thing that happened, yet at moments like this the fact of the accident and Ed's death would bombard her with the force of a tornado. She sometimes wondered how she could go on, how she could remain in Angel Fire as much as she loved the place. What if she really had been driving? It was possible. She had no recollection of it.

Ed's grown children had never told her anything about their plans for Ed's funeral. Of course, she couldn't have gone, wouldn't have gone, even if she hadn't been in the hospital. They had never made any contact with her, except through their attorney saying she could expect to hear from them as they planned to sue her. That was a laugh—what did they think they would get from her? She had no money, no secure cushion for emergencies. Tessa had suggested that perhaps they thought she was going to get a huge settlement from the insurance company, although she might not get anything. If Ed had been driving, Sherry assumed there might be a settlement, but if she had been driving. . . . And that was what scared her. She was one of the thousands of uninsured drivers in New Mexico.

"I guess it's time I talked to a lawyer," she muttered aloud as she pulled the Taos phonebook out of the drawer.

As she skimmed the listing of attorneys she paused and remembered the last time she had done that. It was when she and Bill had decided to divorce after fifteen years of marriage. Reaching that decision had been the greatest struggle of her life, until this situation. At that time she had weighed all the factors, especially those that might affect Amber, and had opted for the chance of a better life rather than staying in a loveless marriage. She had never regretted that decision, even though her parents had expressed their disappointment in her. When she left the city and moved with Amber to Angel Fire, she knew she had done the best thing for both of them. Sure, she sometimes regretted not having a steady man in her life. That might have changed if Ed had lived, but she didn't want to think about that. She turned her gaze back to the listing of attorneys.

Tuesday morning dawned as a bright and beautiful day, a cloudless sky, temperatures expected in the low 70s. As Roberta passed through the living room on her way to the garage, Al called out his usual comment, "Another day in Paradise, honey." She smiled, blew him a kiss, and headed out the door.

Watching Kay close her front door and come down the steps to the car, Roberta was glad to see that Kay was losing the hang-dog, depressed expression she had worn ever since the accident. The red woven straps of her Chaco sandals matched the bright red top she wore today, and she even smiled as she got in the car.

"You're looking good today," commented Roberta.

"I'm feeling good," Kay admitted. "It's time for me to get on with life. Anyway, Music from Angel Fire starts in a few weeks and I intend to enjoy it as always."

"Good for you." They headed down the mountain to join the others.

Everyone in the Tuesday breakfast group arrived at the same time, and the hum of conversation took off immediately. Annabelle was exclaiming about the motto on Wanda's tee shirt. This time it said, "Keep calm and drink a Margarita."

"I can't imagine you drinking a Margarita, Annabelle, or anything else alcoholic for that matter," said Wanda laughing.

"I may not partake myself," Annabelle admitted, "That doesn't mean I don't understand the wisdom expressed by your shirt."

The group settled themselves around their usual table and sipped coffee while waiting for their breakfast orders to arrive.

Roberta leaned forward and asked, "Tessa, I've been meaning to ask, how is your dad doing? Are things back to normal?"

"Well, yes, back to normal, although his normal is always a little dramatic. He likes his new place, at least for the moment. When I talked to him on the phone yesterday he hinted that he had a new girlfriend. Of course, that's what always gets him in trouble, so we'll see."

"It's a continuing saga, isn't it?" Roberta said. "Listen, before we go our separate ways this morning, I wanted to tell you that Al's birthday is in two weeks. It's his 65th, so I want to do something special. I was thinking of a surprise party, no gifts, or only gag gifts if someone wants to bring something. What do you think?'

"Oh, that's a great idea," said Wanda. "I'm going to Santa Fe later this week and I can get some 'over the hill' decorations at the party store."

"Where will you have it?" asked Annabelle.

"I was thinking of the wine room at the country club. It'll be hors d'oeuvres and cake, so we don't need room for a sit-down meal.

"Will you get Earlene to make the cake?" asked Olivia.

"Of course. No one makes a better cake than Earlene. My problem is, how will I pull off a surprise?"

Everyone was quiet for a moment, thinking. "I know! I know," exclaimed Myra. "You and another couple should go to dinner in the dining room. Have them put you in a back corner table near the doors to the deck. All the party guests can go around through the lounge without being seen, and they'll be waiting in the wine room. Then, whoever is at dinner with you can say they want to show you something in the wine room."

"Myra, that's brilliant. I never thought you could be so devious."

Myra's face shone with pride. "Actually, I always wanted to be a spy."

"Now, remember," cautioned Roberta. "This has to be a surprise." The friends all smiled and nodded.

"Did you really want to be a spy, Myra?" asked Wanda.

"Yes, because who would ever suspect me? I could get by with anything."

"That is until someone asked if you were a spy. I can't imagine you lying. You'd probably say, 'I cannot tell a lie. Yes, I'm a spy'" said Roberta.

After the group's laughter died down, Wanda asked, "So, what's everyone reading? I hear Jan Karon has a new Mitford book coming out soon."

As avid readers, everyone in the group jumped into the discussion.

"I'm reading a well-written book," said Tessa. "It's called 'A Working Theory of Love'."

"What's it about?" asked Myra.

"It's a little strange. This computer company is trying to develop a computer with intelligence, one that will have a conversation with you. They've programmed it with these detailed diaries of a man who committed suicide. His son works for the company and is working to set up the conversations."

"That is weird," said Myra.

"Well, then, the father and son finally start having real conversations, which apparently they didn't do in real life."

"That certainly was the way it was in my generation," said Annabelle.

"Funny, I was thinking about that yesterday," put in Roberta. "Thinking about how our parents kept so much to themselves. How all of society did. There was never anything about having babies out of wedlock ever mentioned in public, or living together if not married."

"Or gay marriage," said Myra.

Tessa and Olivia looked around at the three older women, who were all nodding in agreement.

"Things have really changed," said Myra. "It's all because of the 60s."

"The 60s?" repeated Tessa.

"Sure. Think about it. We had all those protests about the war in Vietnam, we had the Civil Rights Movement that was making a huge change in our country, and we had the beginning of the women's movement. Young women suddenly began to question their traditional roles, plus they now had the pill. That changed everything."

"When I was growing up the only job options that seemed possible were teacher, nurse, or secretary," said Annabelle.

Olivia nodded. "I've heard that, though that's so hard to imagine."

"It's true," Roberta said. "Aren't you younger women glad for all the trendsetters who forged the way for you?"

Tessa smiled at her. "Sure, but even with progress in some areas, we're still not being smart in other areas, like the environment, like global warming, like pesticides and GMOs, like . . . "

Myra interrupted, "Now, don't start preaching at us, Tessa."

"And why not?" Tessa voice carried an edge of annoyance. "Someone needs to preach until people start to listen."

"You're right, of course," put in Roberta quickly. "Myra only means that with us, you're 'preaching to the choir' because we agree with you. Angel Fire does such a good job of recycling now compared to a few years ago. By the way, have you all signed up to work at the office for Music from Angel Fire yet?"

Everyone nodded enthusiastically. "Dean Calhoun will be manning the office, and she told me that the training will be next week," Annabelle said.

"I may not be able to help as much this year," said Olivia. "I've got several art shows lined up."

"Where will you be going?" asked Annabelle.

"The usual places; Albuquerque, of course; plus Phoenix; Dallas. I've even entered some smaller shows in Roswell and Steamboat Springs."

"Sounds like fun."

"Actually, it's a lot of work and a little fun, meeting new people and, hopefully, selling some paintings."

As conversation slipped into familiar grooves, Wanda leaned close to Roberta and whispered, "You're still the master of changing the subject from dangerous ground, aren't you?'

Roberta simply smiled.

10

Myra plopped her books on the counter, grabbed up her phone and punched in Roberta's number.

As soon as her friend answered, she blurted out, "Bertie, it's definite. I wanted to be the first to tell you."

"Well, hello to you, too, Myra. Now, slow down. What in the world are you talking about?"

"I saw Alma Bock at the library and she told me. There has been a lawsuit filed by Ed's children against Sherry."

"Oh, dear. I hate to hear that. How did Alma know?"

"Doris Weaver told her, and Doris had heard it from Sherry directly, I think. Anyway, there is definitely a lawsuit. Evidently, Sherry has had to get a lawyer."

"What a shame. Poor Sherry. I wish there was something we could do to help her."

"Actually, I've been thinking about that. Maybe we could have a bake sale or something to raise money for her defense fund."

"She's going to need some help, I'm sure. Myra, maybe we shouldn't talk about it at our Tuesday morning breakfast. I don't know how Kay will feel about that. She's come a long way since the accident, and I'd hate to remind her of how much she was hurt by everything that happened."

"Of course, Bertie. I think you're right. I'll organize it by phone."

"If I were you I'd wait until it's public knowledge and then talk to Sherry first."

"I know. I know. You don't need to tell me. Honestly, Bertie!"

Roberta rolled her eyes in exasperation, glad that Myra couldn't see her. "Oh, sorry. Anyway, thanks for letting me know, Myra."

The two finished their conversation and Roberta hung up the phone, a concerned frown on her face. She walked into the living room where Al was sitting in the recliner. He glanced up at her and noticed her expression.

"What's wrong, Bertie?" he asked.

Roberta sighed and plunked down on the couch. "Oh, Al, it's so sad. Ed's children are filing a law suit against Sherry. It's definite. Poor Sherry. Even if nothing comes of it, having to go through a trial, to go to court and relive the whole thing. I can't imagine how hard that will be."

Al put down the paper and shook his head. "It will be hard, no question about it."

"I wish there were something we could do to help her. She's worked so hard her whole life to raise that daughter by herself and make a good life here. And, in a moment, because of an unexpected event, everything has changed."

"Bertie, hon, you've spent your life trying to make things better for people, to fix everything, and that's an impossible thing to do. Some things you simply can't make better."

Roberta looked at her husband with a wan smile. "But I want to, Al. I really want to."

He shook his head and picked up the paper again. Roberta gave another sigh, got up from the couch and went into the kitchen to begin making lunch.

The breakfast group had decided to meet at Annie's Coffee Shop that week and, at the usual time, they all gathered around the long, rectangular table.

Roberta waited until they were all seated, then announced, "Well, I've got everything set for the surprise party for Al. Do you all have it on your calendars for a week from Saturday?"

They all nodded. Wanda lifted a bag from under her chair. "I got some cute things at the party store," she said. She began pulling them from the bag; a package of sixty-fifth birthday balloons, a table runner and napkins, flashing candles, and a centerpiece all proclaiming 'Happy 65th Birthday.' "Here's the best thing. It's what Robert and I will be giving Al for his gift." She proudly displayed a tee shirt that said "Made in 1949. All Original Parts".

"That's perfect," declared Roberta.

"I'll never forget a party a friend gave for her husband's sixtieth birthday," said Annabelle. "She sent out invitations that it was a wake. When you got there, she had the chairs set up in rows, facing a coffin. It was so creepy!"

"That sounds awful," said Myra. "What did you do for the party?"

"Well, once everyone got there—she was playing this somber music while waiting for everyone to arrive—she had it like a roast where everyone said things about her husband. It did get funny after a while. Then we had refreshments. Honestly, it was the strangest party I've ever been to."

"You can never tell what you people in Dallas will do," said Tessa, and the group smiled in agreement.

"Speaking of parties, said Wanda. "I went to a fun party last Halloween. Instead of dressing in a costume, you were supposed to come dressed as what you wished you might have been, and everyone had to guess what it was you had wanted to be. You could have come as a spy, Myra."

"I would have come in a choir robe," said Annabelle. "That would have been the closest I ever got to singing in a choir."

Wanda smiled. "The cleverest one was this one guy, a short man. He was dressed as a handyman with a tool belt & was carrying a toolbox with several rulers stuck upright in the sand."

"So, what did he want to be?" asked Roberta, a puzzled look on her face.

"He wanted to grow a few inches. Get it?" said Wanda.

Everyone laughed and admitted that was pretty clever.

Sherry looked up from the computer as someone tapped on her office door.

"Come in," she called, but when she saw the state trooper, Officer Thornton, enter her office, she wished she could have pretended she wasn't there.

"Sorry to bother you," he said. "I need to find out what you've remembered about the accident." He pulled out his notebook and pen and looked at her expectantly.

Sherry sighed and leaned back in her chair. "I really can't tell you much more. I've had a few little things come back to me, although I don't think they'll help at all."

"Any little detail might be useful. What can you remember?"

"It's only unimportant things. I remember I picked out my New Mexico Lobos cap to wear that morning because Ed is . . . was . . . an LSU fan." She felt that familiar pain in her chest and throat when she had to face the fact of Ed's death. "We had lunch at Doc Martin's and then we had some errands we were going to do. I can't remember what they were, though. No doubt Walmart was one of them as that is always on my list. I don't know for sure. I remember it was a beautiful, sunny day. That's about it, officer. I'm sorry."

"I will be called to testify at the hearing. It's important that I have as many details as possible."

Sherry's heart began to race even faster. "Oh, yes. The hearing. I guess I have to prove I wasn't driving. How can I do that?" The expression on her face conveyed all her fears and frustration.

"Actually," the trooper said, pocketing his pad, "I believe the issue will be that they will have to prove that you *were* driving and, so far, no one has come forward saying that they saw you at the wheel. That's what it would take." He touched the brim of his hat, turned, and let himself out of the office.

Sherry didn't move for several moments. She reached for the tissue box and wiped away the few tears that had escaped down her cheeks.

She turned back to her computer as the door opened again and Hannah came in the office.

"Hi, Sherry. I was wondering if you had any more house cleaning assignments for me?"

Sherry scrolled through her computer listings. "Here's one for tomorrow." She copied the information on a pad, tore off the sheet and handed it to Hannah. She unlocked the drawer and gave Hannah the house key.

"We haven't really had a chance to visit since I've been back. Tell me how everything is going," Sherry said, gesturing for Hannah to have a seat.

Hannah slipped into the chair by Sherry's desk. "Well, we're doing OK. Shandra and I are putting away every cent we earn to go toward her college fund."

"Oh, where is she working this summer?"

"She's got a job at Zeb's and she babysits or house sits whenever she can."

"It's hard to believe this is her senior year."

Hannah nodded. "That's for sure. If it hadn't been her last year we would have headed back to my home town in Texas to be with my parents after my husband left us as I can hardly make ends meet up here. I sure appreciate your getting me this job, Sherry. It's been a blessing because I can fit it in around my other work schedule."

"I'm glad I could help. I bet it is hard with the rents up here. By the way, where are you . . . "

"Oh, gosh, I didn't realize the time! I've got to run, Sherry." Hannah had jumped up and was heading out the door with the next day's assignment clutched in her hand. "Thanks for this," she called, waving the paper, as she hurried out the door.

Wanda unrolled her mat next to Roberta's at the Community Center. Today her tee shirt proclaimed "We never really grow up. We only learn how to act in public." Smiling, she commented, "I guess the Turks are back. I thought they were going to be gone most of the summer."

"That's what Bobbie said. Why do you think they're back? Did you see them?"

"No. After yesterday's afternoon rain storm I saw the tire marks going into the garage."

"Hmm. I'd be surprised if they were back already. They didn't plan to get here until September. I hope nothing went wrong with their trip."

Wanda looked around and lowered her voice. "You know, Bertie, ever since Olivia asked me about our house, I've had the willies, wondering if someone had broken in or something. I've searched it carefully though, and there's not a thing out of place from when we left."

"Oh, I wouldn't worry about it, I'm sure it was nothing. No doubt it was some odd circumstances that have a logical explanation."

"I hope you're right. I . . . "

The warm-up instructions boomed out from the TV, and conversation was halted until after the exercise session when the group went out for coffee together.

Roberta dropped her keys on the counter as she walked in through the kitchen.

"Hi, hon," she called to her husband.

"Well, it's a good thing you're home. Your friend Kay has called three times in the last hour. She sounds pretty upset. You'd better call her right away."

"Did she say what was wrong?" Roberta asked as she picked up the phone and entered Kay's number.

"Nope. From the tone of her voice I could tell something was upsetting her."

"Kay," Roberta said after Kay had answered on the second ring. "Is something wrong?"

"Yes, Bertie. Something is terribly wrong. Can you come over?"

"Of course, but can't you tell me what it's about?"

"No, I don't want to talk about it on the phone. Can you come over now?"

"Sure. I'll be right over."

It was only moments later that Roberta pulled into Kay's driveway. Kay had the door opened before Roberta even got up the steps.

"Oh, Bertie, thank you for coming," Kay said as she almost pulled Roberta inside. She led the way into the living room and collapsed onto the sofa, a tissue held to her mouth.

"What in the world is the matter? Is it Heather or the boys?"

"No, nothing like that." Kay looked at her friend, her face blotchy from crying. "I've learned that Ed's family is suing Sherry. The person who told me said the only way Sherry might lose the case is if someone comes forward and testifies that they saw Sherry driving that day."

Roberta nodded. "Yes, that's what I understand."

"Well, that's just it. I did. I saw Sherry driving!"

11

Roberta sat back and felt a chill run through her body. "You what?"

"It's true. I saw them, and Sherry was getting in the driver's seat. I didn't think about it at the time because I was so shocked at seeing them together. Oh, Bertie, what am I going to do?"

"But you never said anything about it."

"I wasn't thinking about who was driving. Don't you see? I was so upset about them, about realizing I had lost Ed and then, after the accident, well, I only could think about Ed's death."

"Oh, Kay."

"Then all of a sudden this morning, it hit me. I pictured how I had seen them and I realized I had seen Sherry get in the driver's side. Now I don't know what to do. Do I tell the police? Do I testify against Sherry?"

Roberta shook her head. "This is so hard. I can't imagine how you must be feeling. Kay, you have to do the right thing. If you have information about the accident you need to report it."

Kay looked at Roberta, her eyes full of anguish. "But is that the right thing? It won't make any difference about the accident. Ed will still be dead. If I testify it will, however, make a difference for Sherry. She could lose everything."

"Yes. You know the truth. If you don't tell, it's concealing evidence. And that is wrong. I don't think you have any choice."

Kay got up and paced to the window and back. "You know what people will say, though. They'll say I'm doing it to hurt Sherry because of Ed and our . . . our relationship. They'll think I'm doing it out of spite."

Roberta remained silent.

"They will, and you know it. I won't be able to face anyone in this town." Kay sat down and buried her face in her hands. "Now, when I finally felt I could get on with my life. Why did this have to happen? Why?" Kay's shoulders shook with the sobs.

Roberta put her arm around her friend. She tried to think of something comforting to say, but no words came to her. Kay was right. What she described was exactly what people would think.

Finally, Kay's tears slowed and she sat back. "You see why I needed you here? I can't talk to Heather about it. She'd encourage me to go after Sherry, then move to Las Cruces to be near them. I don't want to do that yet. I love Angel Fire. I love my life here. I don't want to leave."

"And we don't want you to leave. Kay, those factors don't change anything. The bottom line is you know the truth as to who was driving, and you need to come forward with that information."

Kay took a deep breath. "I know," she said. "Would you come with me, come to the police station with me?"

"I will, of course. Why don't you call the chief and tell him you have some information about the accident and could someone come by your house so you could share that information?"

"Do you think they would do that? Come here? Not make me go to the police station?"

"It's certainly worth a try. Why don't you call them now? I'll stay with you."

Kay nodded. "Thank you, Bertie. You're a true friend." She paused. "Do you think I . . . I wonder if maybe I should tell Sherry? I don't think I could face her."

Roberta shrugged. "That would be pretty hard, even though it seems like it would be fair to let her know."

"Would you go tell her for me?"

"Me? Oh, gosh, Kay. I don't want to." Roberta grimaced. That's about the last thing she would ever want to do. On the other hand, she hated to have Sherry blindsided by the news. "I guess I could do that if I had to. Why don't we see what the chief says first, OK?"

Olivia loaded the last of the paintings she had planned to take to the Phoenix show and closed up the back of her Bronco with a sense of satisfaction. She was bringing some of her best work, she thought, plus she had been able to finish a number of smaller paintings that should sell well. She went back inside and gathered up her suitcase, purse, and water bottle.

After placing them in the car she went back inside one last time. She entered her studio and looked around carefully. *Have I taken all the paintings I should?* she wondered to herself. There were still a good number of them propped against the walls. She had been able to get so much painting done in the past year. There were so many locations that had come to mean a lot to her, and they had served as inspiration; several places on the road to Ocate, two special undeveloped spots up in the Aspens section, and the beaver ponds on the way to Mora. And, of course, there were the Spanish churches. Everyone seemed to like her paintings of those sacred places. She loved painting the pure simplicity of their strength, and hoped that showed in each rendition.

"Well," she said aloud, straightening her shoulders. "This isn't getting me to Phoenix." She glanced around one last time and left, locking the door behind her.

Roberta went out onto the deck and sat quietly waiting while Kay made the phone call to the police chief. Moments later Kay came out and stood at the railing gazing at the peaceful scene in front of her. Chickadees and Nuthatches pecked around her bird feeders, as well as Juncos and Finches, flying off when the Steller jays swooped in.

"Well?" asked Roberta.

Kay sighed and turned toward her friend. "Well, it will have to wait for a while. It's the state police who have jurisdiction for some reason, so we have to wait for a state trooper to come over. The Chief said he'd pass on the word to them that I have information, and then he'll call me when they are coming."

"So, we just have to wait, I guess," said Roberta.

Kay nodded. "And with every waiting hour I'll get more and more nervous, and wonder what I should have done." She wandered over and sat in the chair next to Roberta.

"Did they indicate when the trooper would come over; today, next week?"

"He didn't say. I don't know if I need to stay home and wait for the call, or what. How did I get into this mess?" Kay sat back in her chair and closed her eyes. "Honestly, Bertie, if Ed weren't dead, I'd like to wring his neck!" What started out as a rueful chuckle deep in her throat soon bubbled into bitter sobs.

Roberta pulled her chair closer and silently patted Kay's back.

"This whole thing has been so hard! When I think I'm OK about our relationship, I think about Ed being dead and the end is so final. And now, this! Having to testify in court. Being the one to ruin someone else's life! It's too much, Bertie! It's too much to bear!"

"I know it must be," Roberta said softly. "I know."

The two continued to sit on the deck, waiting for whatever was to come.

Al stood in front of their bedroom mirror muttering under his breath as he struggled with his tie. "I don't see why I have to wear this darn thing, Bertie. No one else in Angel Fire wears one."

"Oh, honestly, Al. Stop complaining. Dave and Pat Pangrac were nice enough to ask us out for your birthday dinner at the club. The least you could do is look presentable."

"I can look presentable without a tie. Anyway, I should get to choose whether or not to wear a tie. It's my birthday, after all."

Roberta stopped fastening her earrings and looked at her husband. She had to smile. "All right, don't wear a tie. I guess the world won't end if you don't."

Al went over and gave her a quick peck on the cheek. "That's why I love you, hon. You will occasionally listen to reason."

She arched an eyebrow at him. "Only occasionally?"

"Let's go," Al said, ignoring her comment. "We don't want to be late."

As the two couples finished their dinner, sat back, and put their napkins on the table, Dave said, "I saw an amazing thing in the wine room last week. I wanted to be sure and show you all tonight. Let's slip in there on our way out."

The four rose and made their way around the corner of the dining room. It was all Roberta could do to keep for grinning. She was glad she was behind Al.

Dave opened the door and stood back for Al to enter. The shouts of "Surprise" made Al jump back. His glance took in the room full of laughing friends, and his heart beat a little faster. He turned to Roberta. "You sneaky thing," he murmured as she gave him a hug. "I'll get you for this." His smiling, pleased countenance, however, belied the seriousness of the threat.

When Roberta picked up Kay on Tuesday morning the first thing Kay said as she got in the car was, "I still haven't heard a thing back from the Chief."

"Well, I guess they're in no hurry about getting your information. When is the trial, anyway?"

"I've heard it won't be for months," Kay answered. "I certainly hope no one talks about it at breakfast today."

Roberta smiled. "You know we can keep enough conversation going so we can avoid that topic. I brought a couple of books to pass around, and you know we can always get a good conversation going about books."

When Kay and Roberta entered the coffee shop the conversation was already going strong. After placing their orders the two sat down and Roberta asked, "What are you all laughing about?"

Tessa grinned. "It's my dad again. He's up to his old tricks."

"What's he done now?" Roberta said.

"I was talking to him on the phone Sunday, and he was telling me that he had a new girlfriend. He thought they had a relationship, then she told him she had become engaged to someone."

"Oh, my," said Kay. "Did he get in another fight?"

"No, this is even crazier. I asked my brother to check about it when he went to visit. It turns out the woman was the twenty-something activities director! My brother went to talk to her and she said that my dad had developed this fantasy about the two of them. She assured my brother that it was all in my dad's mind. She said she was working with the psychologist to see how to handle it. Can you imagine?" Tessa shook her head.

"Well," said Roberta, "I don't know your dad, but from your other stories, I can believe it."

The group's laughter was interrupted by the arrival of their breakfast orders. Annabelle commented that they always ordered the same things; she had the breakfast muffin, Wanda got the breakfast burrito, Kay had a Danish pastry, Roberta's was bacon and eggs, Tessa had granola, and Olivia, who was absent that day, would have had pancakes.

"We are all creatures of habit, aren't we?" said Roberta.

"Absolutely. In church we always sit in the same place. What would we do if some stranger sat in our seat?"

"Hopefully, sit next to them and greet them," said Roberta.

Wanda set down her coffee. "Listen, I have a great idea. I was talking to Karen Pettersen yesterday, and we got in a discussion about how good we felt after a day at Ojo Caliente. What do you say to planning a trip over there soon?"

Everyone nodded their agreement, and the conversation was abuzz with comments and recollections of days soaking in the hot mineral baths and getting massages.

"Though you know it will have to wait until after the music festival," said Annabelle. "Everything has to stop during those few weeks."

"And the concerts start this Friday," reminded Tessa. "We'll really need those relaxing waters after all we have to do for Music, right? Let's plan on going the first week in September."

Kay's glance caught Roberta's. *How would the knowledge that she was testifying against Sherry have changed things by then?* she wondered.

12

Sherry felt an odd sense of freedom now that she had a walking cast. Still, finding clothes to wear that she could get over the big black boot was a challenge. That morning she had pulled out an old pair of boot-cut jeans that she hadn't worn since she went out two-stepping at Colfax Tavern. Looking at them as she slipped them on made her feel nostalgic for good times like that. She wondered if she could ever have such fun filled and carefree evenings again. How could she ever do that after Ed's death, especially if she had been the one responsible?

Forcing herself to put such thoughts away, she continued to get ready for work. This had been a busy summer for rentals of the properties she was managing. She was glad each time she could give Hannah an extra cleaning assignment. *I don't know how she and Shandra are managing. The costs of college looming ahead for them next year must be really daunting. With rent in Angel Fire so high, it's got to be hard.*

Sherry drove carefully down to the real estate office. She wound her way past dozens of mountain bikers getting ready for the next weekend's big downhill mountain bike championship. That had become a popular event in Angel Fire, although Sherry couldn't imagine enjoying flying down a mountain, bouncing over rocks and roots, trying to maintain control of something as flimsy as a bicycle. *Well, to each his own, as they say. It's really been good for Angel Fire.*

As she settled at her desk and clicked on her computer, her boss tapped on her door and came in, shutting the door behind him. "How's everything going, Sherry?"

"Well, if you mean by 'everything' the rentals and property managing, everything's going well. If you mean my life, not so much."

Steve nodded. "I do understand. You know, you only need to say the word if you'd like some extra help."

Sherry smiled at her boss. "I appreciate your keeping the job open for me, and the offer of extra help. I'm managing fine. I have a good system in place so it's pretty easy to keep up with everything as long as I can get to my computer."

Steve stood and turned to go. "Just checking." He reached the door and paused, as if to make another comment, then waved his farewell and left.

Sherry sat a moment in the enfolding silence. Did she really have things under control? As far as her job was concerned, she felt confident. The problem was the rest of her life. She looked at her computer for a moment, then leaned back her chair and stood. She stretched her arms up, and moved her head from side to side as she tried to work out the kinks that had formed in her neck. She walked to the window, leaned against the sill, and gazed at the ski mountain jutting up behind the office building.

She wasn't thinking of how it would feel swooshing down the mountain on skis, cold air brushing her cheeks, though. Instead her thoughts wandered back to when she was a teenager with all her life ahead, full of possibilities. She remembered the magic of prom night, the first kisses, the secrets shared. She thought of her first job at the insurance company, where she had met her ex-husband, Bill, and of falling in love and dreaming of happily ever after. What had happened to all of that? What had happened to the promises life had held back then?

She pushed away from the window sill. As she went back to her desk she thought of the struggles Hannah was going through and muttered to herself, "Well, I'm sure not the only one with problems, am I?"

The Tuesday morning group was humming with conversation about the opening Music from Angel Fire concert the Friday before.

"I didn't quite know what to make of that saxophone quartet," said Myra.

Wanda nodded (today her tee shirt proclaimed, "Without music, life would B^b" in honor of the music festival, she had already announced.) "Yeah, that Donald Sinta Quartet was different. I was amazed at their talent. Who knew that saxophones could sound like that?"

"I'm so looking forward to seeing everyone again. After all these years, it always feels like old home week to see these wonderful musicians who have become friends," said Annabelle.

Nods all around as they divided up their usual dishes.

"When does Olivia get back?" asked Kay.

Tessa smiled. "She should get in this evening. She texted me that this was one of her best shows ever."

"Oh, good," said Roberta. "Tessa, where have you been hiking this week?"

"Wheeler Peak. One of my favorite hikes, but not that easy. When we got to the top there was a little rain, which actually became sleet. We saw Rosalie Turner's husband, Frank, and their twelve-year old grandson, Kit, there. Frank looked like he was about to die. They bragged that they were the oldest and youngest up there that day."

"Well, good for them. OK, we haven't talked about books today. Who's read something you can recommend?"

Annabelle wiped her mouth daintily. "Becky Jones lent me Barbara Kingsolver's book, "Flight Behavior." I'm not too far into it. So far I think it's pretty good." She didn't have to wait for other comments, and, as usual, the group managed to break into small conversations and all seemed to talk at once.

Roberta looked around at her group of friends and marveled, as she often did, about how such a diverse group of people could end up in that little mountain town and share their lives in such a unique way. She glanced at Kay who was caught up in a disagreement with Myra about the merits of a book they both had read. *How will Kay handle the difficulties that lie ahead for her?* she wondered. *How will we ALL handle it?*

Olivia pulled into her driveway as the late afternoon sun moved across the mountain. She unloaded the few paintings left from the successful show and carried them into her studio. As she straightened up and looked around, she had the eerie feeling that something was different. Her tubes of paints were lined up as she had left them, her brushes, rags, and solvents were all in order.

She turned slowly, looking all around. The paintings she had left behind were still stacked against the wall. *Or are there fewer than I thought I left?* she wondered. She walked to each section and flipped through the canvasses. Her still life paintings of the pottery were all there, as were the scenes of the beaver pond. There were her aspen scenes, or had she left more?

"I need to be more professional and keep an inventory," she muttered out loud. "Either that or I need to go ahead and admit myself to an old folk's home." She did worry about her memory and the onset of dementia ever since her mother had started to show the signs of early Alzheimer's. She didn't like to think about that. Her parents were too young to have such problems.

Olivia thought back to her growing-up years in California. She had been so fortunate to have a happy, carefree childhood with parents who encouraged her brothers and herself to become whatever they wanted to be, to follow whatever path was right for them. So unlike Tessa's childhood.

Their home on the outskirts of Riverside had been the gathering place for the neighborhood kids. That continued after her family had moved to Albuquerque. Being the youngest, and the only girl, Olivia knew she had been indulged, yet as an adult she was grateful for that background. She knew that was why she had been free to follow her artistic nature. That her short marriage after college hadn't worked out no longer filled her with regret. She actually enjoyed being on her own with no one to be accountable to. She had always enjoyed her nieces and nephews, although she had seen little of her eldest brother's sons since they had started college in Albuquerque.

She walked out of her studio as she thought about her family. She was tired from the art show and the long drive back to Angel Fire. Instead of setting up an inventory system for her paintings or worrying about losing her memory, she decided to pour herself a glass of wine and sit on her patio savoring the beauty of the mountains around her. Settling into her favorite chair with a glass of Pinot Grigio, Olivia sighed. Life was good.

In the end Kay decided she'd prefer go to the police station, which was really an office in the building behind the post office, rather than have a state-police car and Angel Fire police car in her driveway. After all, Angel Fire was a small town. No telling what people would say about such cars at her house. She shuddered to think about it. It was going to be bad enough when everyone heard that she was testifying against Sherry.

Roberta came by to get Kay, and they headed down the mountain.

"You look very nice today," Roberta said, noting how well Kay's jewel-green top looked with her green eyes.

"Thanks, Bertie. And thanks for going with me today. I've been so nervous ever since the Chief called and said the state trooper would be here today. I want to try to appear calm and rational. I don't want them to think I'm doing this out of spite."

"I'm sure they won't even think about that. Don't worry. You'll do fine. Just tell them what you saw."

The two friends rode in silence the rest of the way. Roberta pulled into a parking place next to the state trooper's car.

"Well, I guess they're ready for me," Kay said with a grimace. The two got out and entered the office.

The Chief came forward, greeted them and led them into his office. "This is Officer Thornton," he said introducing the tall, stern man in uniform who rose to meet them.

"Thank you for coming, Mrs. Tucker," the officer said as he gestured toward the two chairs for them to sit down.

Kay and Roberta sat, and Kay licked her lips. Her mouth had suddenly gone dry.

The Chief smiled at her. "There's nothing to be nervous about, Kay. We only want to hear about what you actually saw the day of the accident."

Officer Thornton took out his pad and pen and also set a recording device on the desk. "You don't mind if we record this, do you, Mrs. Tucker?"

Kay glanced at Roberta, and then looked back at the officer. "No. No, I guess not."

Officer Thornton turned on the machine, stated who was in the room, referenced the accident, and the date and time. "Now, Mrs. Tucker," he began. "We understand that you remember seeing Ed Wilson and Sherry Sullivan on the day of the accident, is that correct?"

"Yes, that's right. I saw them."

"Would you please tell us where you saw them and approximately what time it was?"

Kay cleared her throat. "I was in the parking lot at Walmart in my car. It was about 3:30 or 4 in the afternoon. I'm pretty sure of the time because I'd had a 2:30 appointment. It lasted about an hour, and then I was going to do some errands."

"So, you saw them in the parking lot, then did your errands and then returned to Angel Fire?"

Kay darted a look at Roberta again. "No. I . . . I decided to go right home after I had seen them."

Officer Thornton continued making notes in his pad. He asked, "And why was that?"

Kay sighed deeply and slumped in her chair. "Is that really relevant, Chief?" she asked looking up the Chief.

Officer Thornton answered instead. "Ma'am, we won't know what is relevant until we know everything. Please continue."

"I . . . I was upset at seeing Ed and Sherry together. Well, you see," she paused. "Ed had been a special friend." Kay's face burned red, and she shifted uncomfortably in her chair. Roberta reached over and patted her arm. It was clear that the motion didn't escape Officer Thornton's attention.

"So, you were sitting in your car in the parking lot and you saw the two of them. What exactly did you see?"

"I saw them walk out of the store. Each of them was carrying a bag. They walked to that old jeep of Ed's and Sherry got in the driver's side."

"You saw Sherry Sullivan get in the driver's seat?" Officer Thornton asked looking up at Kay.

"Yes."

"You're absolutely certain you saw Mrs. Sullivan get in the driver's side?"

"Yes. Yes, I am absolutely certain."

"Did they leave the parking lot first, or did you?"

"I left first. I left right away."

"Did you see them after that?"

"No." Kay bit her lower lip. "I never saw Ed again." She seemed to draw into herself. Roberta wished she could do something to help Kay at this difficult time. She knew there really wasn't anything she could do.

The Chief spoke up, "I think that's all we need, Bob, don't you? Kay has been a helpful witness."

"Yes, you have been helpful, Mrs. Tucker. Thank you for coming in. Please get in touch if you remember anything else." He stood and shut off the recorder.

Kay looked around as if to make sure she was actually free to go. She and Roberta stood and shook hands with the two men and headed out to the car.

As Roberta looked in the mirror to back out, Kay wailed, "I thought I would die back there! I don't think I can do that if I have to do it in court. Bertie, what am I going to do?"

Sherry saved the latest information on her computer and shut it down. She was tired and ready to go home. She still hadn't bounced back to her usual self, and a full day at her desk was hard. She was glad she loved her job, and especially now with the stress of facing the details of the accident and the court case looming in the future. If she didn't have her job and her friends to distract her she probably would sink into depression, she often thought.

She wouldn't let herself get depressed. She was determined about that. It was a tragedy that Ed had been killed. She had liked him and enjoyed his company, although they had not really had enough time to develop a serious relationship. *What would have happened if there hadn't been the accident and I had gone to Denver with him?* She never really knew if she would have gone with him or not. She knew of his reputation as a "ladies' man", yet it would have been tempting.

Sherry shook her head to stop those thoughts. She didn't want to think about Ed, about that day in Taos, about the accident. She had enough things to worry about with the business of looking after other people's homes and keeping up with renting them.

As she was gathering her purse to leave, her cell phone rang. She glanced at the caller ID and saw it was the attorney she had hired to represent her.

"Yes, Phil?" she said quickly.

"Hi, Sherry, how are you doing?"

"I'm OK. What's up?"

"I," he hesitated. "I'm afraid I have some bad news. I understand that there is some new evidence. Someone has come forward saying they saw you get in the driver's seat that day."

Sherry sank back into her chair, an icy shiver going through her body. Now, she knew, there was no hope left for her.

13

The Music from Angel Fire Festival filled the valley with the amazing sounds of Bach, Shostakovich, Vivaldi, all the favorites and even some less often performed such as Farina, Albinoni, and Hindemith. The concerts, the receptions, and the parties associated with the festival filled almost three weeks, and, as usual, everyone seemed surprised that September had rolled around so quickly. The fields of wildflowers were shifting from the purple of the penstemon and white yarrow to the asters and the phlox. Time moved on and the seasons began to change.

The Tuesday Breakfast Group continued to meet at Annie's Coffee Shop and always found plenty to talk about.

"So many of our seasonal friends are getting ready to leave," moaned Olivia one Tuesday in early September. "I had to say good bye to Jackie Covey on Sunday."

Myra nodded. "And Sylvia Hornback is going next week as well as Jan Mika."

"I don't know how all these people can stand to leave. Fall is the prettiest time of year here."

"As well as summer," put in Wanda. Her tee shirt today said "Wine drinkers make grape lovers."

"And winter," Roberta reminded them.

"Yeah, and then there's spring," said Tessa laughing. "Spring, which we all call 'mud season'. But, ladies, time is a passing, and we were going to Ojo Caliente one day. We need to get that planned. How about next week?"

"Sounds good to me," said Annabelle. "My aches and pains feel better after a day there. Which day shall we go?"

"How about Thursday?" suggested Myra.

Several pulled out their calendars from their purses, and Tessa and Olivia consulted their iPhones. Everyone agreed Thursday would be perfect. Of course, thinking about the healthful benefit of the hot mineral waters made everyone start talking about their aching joints and muscles.

"Honestly," said Annabelle. "Listen to us! We sound like a bunch of old-timers trying to play 'Can You Top This.' Sure, we all have problems. Who doesn't? We're so lucky to be able to get up every morning in this beautiful place and hike, golf, swim, or simply look at the mountains."

"You're right," said Roberta. "We shouldn't ever complain."

Myra glanced over at Kay. "You've sure been quiet lately, Kay. Are you doing OK?"

"Of course. I'm fine. I have a lot on my mind, I guess." She smiled wanly.

"Well, remember you're among friends here." Myra gave her a sympathetic smile.

Roberta could almost feel Kay bristling, so she commented, "You know, thinking about going to Ojo Caliente, we ought to see if Vernett Safford wants to go, too. She'll be starting her preschool any time, and she's recovering from that broken foot. It might be exactly what she needs."

"Sure, call her," the group agreed.

"I'll call Linda Nelson," said Annabelle. "The arsenic pool would do her arthritis a world of good."

"Anything new with your dad, Tessa?" asked Roberta.

Tessa shook her head. "No, everything seems to be quiet for now. Actually, I think he's really beginning to fail. My brother said that my dad seemed to be slipping more and more into dementia."

"I worry about that with my mom, too," said Olivia. "I was with them last week and she seemed fine, but I never feel secure that she'll be that way the next time I visit."

Annabelle looked from one to the other. "When we're young, we don't think about all the hard things that can happen in life, do we? Every one of us has experienced the pain from loss or worry over loved ones. I think the important thing about growing older is that we learn how to keep going and we work to still find something to hope for, to be thankful for."

The group of friends sat silently for a moment, each acknowledging a particular pain in their life, even though, more importantly, recognizing the thread of joy that they were still able to find.

Myra cleared her throat. "Well, that's a pretty serious note to leave on, isn't it? Does anyone have any light-hearted comments before we go?"

"Wanda, tell us what another one of your tee shirts says. Which one are you planning for tomorrow?"

Wanda chuckled. "I can't decide between 'Sometimes I open my mouth and my mother comes out' or 'With age comes oldness'. What do you all vote for?"

"Definitely the mother one. That is so true," said Kay. They all smiled as they began gathering purses, keys, and the latest books they were passing around, and headed out the door.

Roberta and Kay had barely started the drive home when Kay burst out, "That Myra! She drives me crazy. She wants to get me to talk about my seeing Ed and Sherry, and I'm not going to do it! I will NEVER talk to her about it, or anything personal for that matter." She slumped in her seat, her arms crossed against her chest.

"Oh, I know what you mean. We need to remember that Myra really has a good heart. She means well." Roberta glanced at Kay.

"I'm not so sure about that. She only wants to find people in difficult times so she can take them one of her damn casseroles."

Roberta had to bite her lip to keep from laughing. “Well, I can tell you’re really mad because you’ve used your once-a-year swear word.”

“Humpf,” Kay muttered. “I might start using it more often. It made me feel better.”

Olivia drove home through Black Lake and up the dirt road toward her house. Pulling around a curve she saw Susan Stuart and Carolin Sanders out on their daily walk. She pulled beside them and stopped the car. “How are you doing?” she asked through her open window. “I haven’t seen you in a while.”

“We’re fine,” answered Susan. “How was your latest show?”

Olivia smiled. “It was the best one yet. I sold almost everything. Now, I’ve really got to get busy and paint a lot more. My next big show will be in Denver in November.”

“Will you have your nephew come and house sit for you again?” Carolin said.

“My nephew? House sit? What do you mean?”

“We met him when we walked by your house one day while you were in Phoenix. We had forgotten you were going to be gone then, and we stopped in to say hi. Your nephew came to the door and said he was there house-sitting for you.”

“No, I hadn’t asked my nephew to come. Are you sure he said he was my nephew? What did he look like?”

Carolin and Susan looked at each other. “Well,” began Susan, “he was maybe 5’10” or 11”, dark hair, nice looking. Of course, there were tattoos and piercings.”

Carolin added, “He looked to be college age, wouldn’t you say, Susan?”

Susan nodded.

Olivia shook her head. “That sounds like Tony, my oldest brother’s son. He’s at UNM now. Although I didn’t know he was coming up here.”

“We’ve seen the same car there before when you’ve been gone to shows, Olivia. We assumed you always had him come look out for your house.”

"That's strange, but, believe me, I'll get to the bottom of it. I'll be heading to my brother's in Albuquerque this weekend. Thanks for telling me."

The three stayed talking for a short time then waved their goodbyes. Olivia drove home feeling unsettled. *Why was Tony up here? Did he get a key from his dad? What is going on?*

Roberta came into the living room where Al was watching CNN. "Honestly," she said, plopping down on the couch. "That Myra can be so annoying."

Al smiled at his wife. "Tell me something new."

"She wants so badly to have the latest gossip that she says the rudest things to people. She wants Kay to give her all the dirt about seeing Ed and Sherry. Of course, it's all over town that Kay saw Sherry driving the day of the accident. Myra is pushing to hear it from Kay herself."

"It may surprise you to know, hon, that that was not the subject of discussion at our men's breakfast."

"It wasn't?" asked Roberta looking up at him.

"Nope. This time of year, do you think we talked about anything except golf and football?"

Roberta rolled her eyes. "I should have known."

"And we try never to talk about politics," Al said with a chuckle.

"Good plan. Seriously, Al, I don't know how Kay will survive when the case comes to trial. She was a mess after we talked to the state trooper. It's going to be so hard on her."

Al turned off the TV. "I have a good idea. Let's go to the driving range or something. Get your mind off worrisome things. Besides, it's too beautiful a day to be indoors."

She smiled at him as he got up and offered his hand to pull her up from the couch. "That's why I've loved you all these years, you have such good ideas."

"Oh, I've had lots of good ideas for us over the years, darlin'," he said, giving her a devilish leer and putting an arm around her shoulders as they left the room.

"Dirty old man," Roberta muttered. But she kept smiling.

Thursday dawned bright and beautiful, a typical fall day for northern New Mexico, the sky deep blue, the air fresh and crisp. Six of the seven friends met in Lowe's parking lot at eight o'clock sharp.

"Can't Olivia ever be on time?" muttered Myra to no one in particular.

"I'm sure she'll be along in a minute," said Roberta. "Ah, here she comes." She pointed to the blue Bronco pulling into the parking lot.

The group divided up into two cars. Kay, Myra and Annabelle rode with Roberta, and, Olivia, and Wanda climbed into Tessa's PT Cruiser.

Wanda, whose tee declared "I have not yet begun to procrastinate," began the conversation as they headed out by saying, "I wonder what they're talking about in the other car. Do you think Myra is finding out who might need a casserole in the valley or is she getting Kay to open up about what she saw before that accident?" Her throaty chuckle bubbled out.

Olivia smiled. "We shouldn't laugh about that. Poor Kay. What a terrible thing for her. As if the whole business wasn't sad enough, the fact that she'll have to testify about that day is too much."

"You're right," said Wanda. "I wasn't really laughing about that. I was laughing about how hard Myra tries to get all the latest about everything."

Tessa signaled for a left turn onto Route 64. "Yet who is it we ask when we want to know anything about what's going on in Angel Fire, hmm? That makes us 'enablers' or something, doesn't it?"

Wanda leaned forward from the back seat. "You're beginning to sound like Roberta."

All three laughed. "We know each other so well, don't we?" Wanda reminded them.

The road began its switch-back route to reach the pass. "That was such a terrible accident, though," Olivia said musingly. "What a tragedy on so many levels."

The three rode in silence for a few moments. "This is where they went off the road," said Tessa as they approached a curve.

"Right here? How do you know?"

"Remember, I mentioned that a while back that one day when Jim and I were hiking the Elliott Barker Trail we came to see where the accident happened? It was right afterward so the evidence of the path the jeep followed was still obvious."

"Was the jeep still there?"

"Oh, no. They'd already hauled it out of there."

"That must have been quite a challenge for somebody," Wanda remarked.

"I'm sure it wasn't easy, but that young man from Taos—I don't know his name, Sammy something—has made quite a business of pulling cars out of ditches and pulling wrecked cars from the woods below all these curves."

"Well, that would be a good way to make a lot of money up here," observed Olivia.

"For sure." Olivia's and Wanda's eyes gazed at the fateful spot as they passed it.

Tessa kept her eyes toward the road. *Should I say anything about the pills I found that day?* she wondered. *No, that's a deep, dark secret I'd better forget.*

14

The two cars went through Taos and passed over the gorge bridge. "It's such a beautiful gorge," commented Annabelle. "So sad to think that people actually commit suicide by jumping off this bridge."

Myra nodded. "The governor has asked the Department of Transportation to put phones along the bridge. I suppose that's so people can get help or something."

"That doesn't seem practical at all," said Roberta. "In this age of cell phones, there's plenty of phone access. I don't see why they don't put up a high fence."

"Who knows?" Kay said as they left the bridge behind and turned left on the road to Ojo Caliente. The four relaxed as they drove along. Roberta enjoyed telling them stories of her grandchildren's latest activities. Kay, for one, was glad to have a conversation that did not include anything about the accident.

Thirty minutes later the cars pulled into the parking lot at the hot springs. The seven friends gathered their towels and bags from the cars and headed into the office. After registering and signing up for their massages, they hurried to the locker room to change and begin enjoying the relaxing benefits of the mineral pools.

"Which one first?" asked Tessa.

"Let's start off with mud baths. That's always fun," suggested Wanda.

They took turns sloshing the shower water on their limbs, then went to the huge tub of mud and lathered it generously on arms, legs, and even faces.

"We should take a picture of us and have them put it in the Chronicle." They all laughed at Olivia's suggestion. Of course, each hoped no one would pull out a cell phone and snap a quick picture. It could easily end up on Facebook.

They sat baking in the sun as the mud dried on their bodies. After rinsing off they moved to the mineral hot pools, all in a "whisper zone" so conversation was infrequent and muted. They luxuriated in the feel of the 110-degree mineral water as they let muscles relax, tensions soothe away.

"Too bad Vernett and Linda couldn't come," said Annabelle.

"Yes," agreed Kay. "This would have done them a world of good."

"I'm going on to the arsenic pool," said Myra after a while. "That's supposed to really help arthritis."

Annabelle rose to climb out of the pool. "I'll come with you. Shall we all meet at the restaurant at noon?"

With a plan in place they all moved around the various pools for the rest of the morning. Wrapped in matching terry cloth robes supplied by the resort, they gathered around a table in the restaurant for lunch.

After they all had ordered, Myra said, "I saw that young woman, Hannah the other day. She has a job cleaning the country club besides her job cleaning rental houses. We had a nice, little visit. She and her daughter are both working so hard to put away money for Shandra's college in a year. I have to say, I really admire them both for the way they are working toward their goal."

"Mmm. This isn't the easiest place for working people to save money."

"No, it's not," Tessa agreed. "We're fortunate in that, with the computer age, Jim can continue to be employed by his California company, and we can live wherever we choose."

In this relaxing setting, after a morning in the pools, conversation was lulled. When the food came, the group got even quieter.

Finishing the last bite of her salad, Olivia pushed back her plate. "I'm going to see my brother this weekend in Albuquerque," she began. "Something kind of disturbing has been happening."

The group leaned forward with an expectant air, their attention on Olivia.

"I learned that my nephew Tony has been coming up when I've been away at shows, and he's been staying at my house. No one ever said anything to me about him coming up here. I don't even know if his parents know. What bothers me is why is he coming? Is he bringing a girl up or what?"

"That is disturbing," said Roberta. "Is he the one in college?"

Olivia nodded.

"Maybe he needs a quiet place to get away and study, or at least have a little break," suggested Kay.

"I hope that's the reason. I'm disappointed that he's doing this behind my back. My family members are always welcome at my house, and they know that, so I can't understand why he's been secretive about it."

Annabelle looked at her watch. "Time for my massage. I asked for a masseuse. I don't want any strange man putting his hands on my body." She rose to go.

Wanda chuckled. "I'm hoping for some handsome, young hunk myself."

Al had the grill cleaned and ready when Roberta got home that evening.

"Well, how was it?" he asked.

"It was heaven," she answered. "The weather was perfect, and it was so therapeutic to soak in the pools and get a massage."

"And did the ladies get along all day?"

"Of course. We always get along. Besides, no one brought up anything about the accident or the court case so Kay was able to really relax for a change."

"Do you know when the case will finally get to trial?" he asked.

"No. They told Kay it would be sometime this fall. That's all she knows."

"And she really will have to testify, I guess."

"I'm sure. So far as we know, she's the only witness. It is such a shame. This has been a nightmare in every way for her." Roberta washed her hands at the kitchen sink and brought out the chicken from the refrigerator for her husband to grill.

It had been a busy week for Sherry. A number of people were trying to get in a last trip to the mountains before the summer season finished and the weather cooled off. She was going over her listings and noting where Hannah would need to clean on Sunday.

Sherry stretched her leg out and leaned back in her chair. Now that she only had a short boot to wear she was getting around pretty well, still, sitting at a desk got wearisome. Her leg had not healed completely yet even though the doctor was pleased with her progress.

Her memory was still coming back in flashes. She now remembered when Ed had picked her up that morning. He'd been wearing a blue shirt that matched his eyes so well and khaki shorts. He'd been a handsome man. His smiling face came to her consciousness at surprising times, always leaving her with a stab of sorrow that was like a physical blow. *Why did that accident have to happen? Why?* She had asked herself that a hundred times, a thousand times. There never was an answer. Underneath all that was the even more disturbing question: Was she the driver?

Saturday morning Olivia finished washing her few breakfast dishes and took a peek in her studio on her way to the garage, wishing she could spend an uninterrupted day painting. The light in her studio was perfect this time of year. With a sigh, she turned and continued on to the garage.

She headed her Bronco out of town, onto Route 64, and began the climb to the pass. At the point of the accident that Tessa had pointed out to them, she couldn't help but think about Sherry, Kay, and even Ed. What far-reaching effects there were from the simple act of a deer jumping into the road. The difficulties that lay ahead for Sherry and Kay made her realize that her worries of that day weren't as serious. She relaxed and began to enjoy the drive she loved.

Passing through Rancho de Taos she followed the road to the crest where it swooped down to meet the river. She loved this view of the gorge, so she pulled off into the parking area to savor it. Her imagination let her picture settlers trudging across the plains and coming to this giant chasm, and she tried to put herself in their place, in their thoughts. She had attempted to paint this scene many times, and still hadn't been able to capture the grandeur of the gorge. She felt that it had some mystical quality to it that couldn't be expressed by paint and canvas.

Olivia put the Bronco in gear and started off again. Going along the Rio Grande, she was glad to see there were still a lot of rafters and kayakers. She had done the rafting trip many times with her nieces and nephews, including Tony. Surely their relationship was strong enough that Tony wouldn't have been doing anything harmful at her house. *Even so, I have to know what was going on.*

Two hours later she parked in her brother Michael's driveway. Her sister-in-law, May, greeted her warmly and ushered her out to the back yard where Michael was pulling weeds from their seemingly perfect flower beds. He straightened up and came to greet his sister.

"When you called, you sounded like there was a problem. What's up, Sis?"

Olivia took a seat on the patio and looked from her brother to her sister-in-law. "I hope it's nothing, but I need to get it straightened out. Did you know that whenever I've had a show, Tony has been coming up and staying at my house?"

"You mean he's been house-sitting for you?" asked May.

"No. I never asked him to come, and I didn't know he was there. He's been doing it behind my back. I wouldn't have known about it except some neighbors happened to mention it to me."

Michael and May exchanged a worried look. Michael leaned forward and clasped his hands between his knees. "We," he began, giving May a quick, nervous glance. "We have had some concerns about Tony since he's been at the university. He's always been a good kid. Lately though, we think he's gotten in with some kids that aren't a good influence on him."

"We don't know if he's tried drugs, or what," May said, tears pooling in her eyes. "We don't know what to do."

"Have you talked to him about it?" Olivia asked.

"We've tried. He says there's no problem. He says that we can no longer boss him around."

"Well, he's still under your roof, isn't he?"

May wiped her eyes. "No, not any more. He moved into an apartment off Central with three other guys."

Olivia sat back and thought about what they were telling her. "I just don't see why he would come to my house when I'm not there."

Michael shook his head. "I have no idea. Let me call him and ask him to come over for lunch. We need to confront him or we'll never really know." He fished his cell phone out of his pocket and hit the speed dial for his son. After a short conversation, he disconnected, nodded to the two women and said, "He'll be here in an hour."

Sherry woke late that Saturday morning, glad for a chance to sleep in, although she had plenty of chores waiting for her here at her condo. Her nights had not been easy since the accident, often full of disturbing dreams, and so she never awoke feeling really rested. As the days inched closer to fall and the court hearing, Sherry's nights grew harder. She often woke with a new flash of memory that had come to her during her fitful sleep. She was beginning to be able to piece a lot of that fateful day together. Even so, the part surrounding leaving Taos and the accident was shrouded in a fog.

The phone rang as Sherry was putting away the last of her breakfast dishes. Glancing at caller ID she was pleased to see it was her daughter.

"Amber, how are you?"

"Hi, Mom. We're all fine. How are you doing?"

"I'm managing OK. Being so busy at work helps a lot. Amber, I'm glad you called. I thought of something last night and wondered what you might think about it. You know, I still can't remember about the accident. What do you think about my going under hypnosis and trying to remember that way?"

"Oh, Mom, why would you do that? Why would you want to remember the accident?"

Sherry hesitated. "Because . . . because what if I wasn't driving? Then there's no case against me."

"Sure, except what if you were the driver. Then you're giving Ed's kids exactly what they need to ruin you. Why would you want to do that?"

Her voice caught as tears came to her eyes. "I have to know, sweetheart. I need to know."

When Sherry put down the phone after their conversation going over the pros and cons of her idea, she still didn't know what to do. The accident had wounded her in so many ways. She was healing slowly from the physical injuries. She doubted if she would ever heal from the emotional ones. If she couldn't prove that Ed was driving, she also would never heal from the financial wounds either.

She had heard that it was Kay Tucker who was testifying that she had seen Sherry driving the jeep that day. Sherry understood that Ed and Kay had seen a lot of each other, yet Sherry knew Kay and couldn't imagine that she was making up the story for spite. *Had I really been driving? Not knowing is killing me!*

Since she had been getting flashes of memory back she had started writing an outline of that day, filling in the pieces as she remembered them. Little by little, the day's activities were coming back to her. She got out her notebook and checked it over.

10 a.m. Ed picked me up in his jeep. He brought two cups of his favorite coffee that Raymond Jaramillo roasted in Black Lake. He was wearing a blue shirt and khaki shorts. I was wearing white capris and a red tank top, and my Lobos cap. Ed drove into Taos.

11 a.m. We parked on Bent Street and went to Moby Dickens Book Store, browsed for books.

12 noon – We wandered over to Doc Martin's restaurant. We both had enchiladas. We took a long time over lunch, talking about lots of things: our different backgrounds growing up, our children, etc.

After that things got hazy. Sherry remembered that they were going to do errands. What were they? And what happened after that? Try as hard as she might, she could not remember.

15

Olivia grew more apprehensive as the hour waiting for Tony drew to a close. What could his reason possibly be for staying at her house? Soon they heard a car pull into the driveway and, moments later, Tony bounded in with a big smile on his face.

"I hope you have a big lunch ready, Mom. I'm . . . " He stopped short when he saw Olivia. "Auntie. I didn't know you were here. What brings you off the mountain?" He gave her a hug, then one to his mom and dad.

"Actually, you do, Tony. I need to ask you some questions."

"Why don't we have lunch first?" suggested May. "I have a nice meal prepared and . . .'

Michael held up his hand to stop her. "No, I think we need answers first."

Tony looked from one to another uneasily as they all sat down. "So, what's up?"

Olivia looked Tony directly in the eye. "I want to know why you've been coming to my house when I wasn't there."

"What do you mean? I wasn't at your house."

"Tony, don't you dare lie to us," his father said.

"My neighbors told me you were there while I was in Phoenix at the art show, and that you'd been there when I was at other shows. I want to know why."

"I," Tony began, his face a mask of anguish. "I can't tell you." He hung his head.

"You'd better tell us, and tell us now." Michael's voice was harsh, full of anger.

"Son," May said, "we're your family. You can tell us."

Olivia waited quietly, watching Tony as he struggled with what to do and what to say. She thought of him as a small boy, delighting with her as they hiked in the mountains, finding unusual rocks, sighting deer, coyotes, and sometimes elk. She remembered a painting he had proudly brought to her saying, "I want to be an artist like you, Auntie Livie." What had happened to that boy? Who was this young man in front of her in such obvious distress?

Michael's fists were clenching. "Anthony. Tell us. Now."

Tony looked at his dad. There was a trail of tears on his cheeks. He roughly wiped them away with his arm. "OK. OK. I'll tell you." He took a deep breath. "These guys I lived with. They're not bad guys really. We gambled a lot. We played poker there almost every night. We went to the casino some. I started out doing OK. Then I started losing. This one guy who came to the apartment, he has an uncle. He said this uncle would lend me money until I started winning again, you know?"

"Oh, Tony," May said, shaking her head.

"I don't know, honest, I don't know how it got so bad. I kept losing, and he kept lending me money. Money that I couldn't pay back. Then there was the interest on what I owed him. It kept getting worse and worse. I tried gambling more, hoping I could win some money to pay him, but there was no way I could pay him back. Then he started threatening me."

May gasped as she put a hand to her mouth.

Olivia kept watching Tony, still not understanding where all this was going.

Michael, too, was looking confused. "So, you went to your aunt's house to get away from this guy or what?"

Tony looked at his father, then at Olivia. He shook his head. "No. No." Tears were pouring from his eyes. "I'm sorry, Auntie, I'm sorry. I shouldn't have done it. I don't know what made me do it!"

"Do what?" Olivia asked.

"Steal some of your paintings to sell to get the money to pay him back. I took some of those ones you do of Spanish churches, and some others. I'm sorry! I'm so sorry!"

Before anyone could say a word, Michael was out of his chair, grabbed his son upright and slapped him so hard that Tony fell onto the floor.

"You stole from your aunt! I'm ashamed to call you my son." He stormed out into the back yard, the door slamming behind him.

May stood, looking from her son to where her husband had gone.

Olivia was stunned with the shock of discovery. *The missing paintings. Of course!* She remained sitting, shaking so badly she didn't think she was capable of standing.

Tony came to her chair and knelt down in front of her, sobbing. "Can you ever forgive me? I'm sorry, Auntie. I'm really sorry. I was so scared, though."

Olivia put both hands to her face. Her thoughts were reeling. What should she say? It was unthinkable that Tony would steal from her, and yet, he had. Could she ever forgive him?

May stood weeping, torn between her son and her husband. Olivia glanced at her and said, "Why don't you go to Michael and let Tony and me work this out ourselves?"

May hesitated, then left the room. The silence she left behind was fraught with emotions: anger, grief, heartbreak.

Finally, Olivia put her hand on Tony's shoulder. "Sit here next to me. Let's figure out where we go from here."

Tony slowly got to his feet and sat in the chair next to Olivia, his head still drooping, still unable to meet her eyes.

"So, how long has this gambling been going on?" she asked.

"Ever since my freshman year, even while I was living at home."

"Why didn't you go to your parents? Why didn't you come to me for help?"

Tony shook his head. "I was so ashamed. I couldn't."

"So, you think it was better to deceive us, to steal from me?"

"No. I don't know what I was thinking. I was so scared, you know? I just wanted the problem to go away."

"Are you still gambling?"

Tony's head jerked up and he looked at her directly for the first time. "No! There's no way I would ever gamble for money again."

"And have you paid off what you owe this guy's uncle?"

Tony nodded. "Yes, I got it all paid last week. I never want to see him again."

"Don't you think it would be better if you made other living arrangements?"

"I already have. I've been bunking in a friend's apartment, and when his roommate leaves next week, I can move in."

Olivia nodded her approval. "So, how do you think you can pay back what you stole from me?"

Tony's head was in his hands as he rocked back and forth. "I can't. There's no way I can make up for what I did."

Olivia sat silently for a moment. "I think there is a way to try. First, you'll have to get some kind of part time job and pay me half of whatever you make every payday."

Tony nodded, finally able to look at her.

"Second, you need to do some kind of community service. You find something or your dad will find it, I don't care.

"Third, find some time to come up to Angel Fire and cut and stack the wood I'll need this winter"

"I'll do it, Auntie. I'll do whatever you say. Anything else?"

"Yes. One more thing." Olivia hesitated. "Find some ways to show your parents and me that we can trust you again."

Tony's expression was crestfallen. "How can I ever do that?"

Olivia shrugged. "That's your problem, Tony. Now, I'm going to say goodbye to your parents and head back to Angel Fire. After I'm gone, you try to make some kind of peace with them."

For most of the three-hour drive home, Olivia wondered how Tony and his dad could ever find their way back to each other.

Tessa, Jim, Roberta, and Al met at the parking lot of Lowe's at 7:15 in the morning. Al and Roberta climbed into the backseat of the Garcia's car.

They exchanged greetings and Roberta said, "This is a perfect day to ride the Cumbres and Toltec train." They all agreed as they started out through the canyon. Driving through Taos, they headed north toward the ski area, then turned west and crossed the gorge bridge. Passing the earth-ship house built underground, their conversation turned to what it must be like to live in such a home.

"I don't think I could stand it," said Tessa. "I have to be able at least to see out, even if I can't be outside."

An hour later they pulled into the parking lot for the scenic excursion train. While waiting for the time to depart, they walked to the front of the train and admired the hissing steam engine. The day-long trip got underway, and the four settled in their seats as the train wound its way up the mountain. Once up amid the breathtaking vistas, they wandered out to the open car where a docent was giving all kinds of information about the history of that narrow-gage railroad, the flora and fauna they were seeing, and the geology around them.

Although they had ridden the train many times, they never tired of the incredible views and scenery that the trip provided. It was especially beautiful at this time of year with the aspen beginning to reach their peak golden color.

"I think I love fall best," said Roberta on the way home that evening.

"Even with the grasses and everything all turning brown?" asked Jim.

"Everything doesn't turn brown," said Roberta. "The grass really becomes burnished brass, the cottonwoods are brilliant yellow, the scrub oak is all shades of bronze, the willows are russet, and then other things are burnt sienna or umber or ochre or . . . "

Jim laughed. "OK. Stop. I give up. I thought everything was brown. Obviously, I was wrong."

Roberta turned and smiled at him. "I'm glad you see things my way."

Al chuckled. "That's always wisest, my friend."

Sitting around their usual table at Annie's Coffee Shop, the Tuesday breakfast group sat spellbound as Olivia recounted all that had transpired during the trip to her brother's the weekend before.

Roberta put her hand on Olivia's arm. "You handled that so beautifully. I don't know what I would have said if it had been my nephew. I can't imagine what a shock that was for you."

"I'm still in shock," replied Olivia. "My own nephew, stealing from me. It seems impossible."

"It sounds like he is truly sorry, though," said Myra.

Olivia nodded. "Yes, I think he is. This has really made me realize that I need to set up an accounting system for my paintings. I've never cared anything about the business part of being an artist. I had thought some were missing. I assumed I had taken them to a show, sold them and forgotten to record it. I was beginning to think I was already suffering from dementia."

"I think that many days," said Annabelle.

Wanda smiled. "I have a tee shirt for that."

"I bet you do," Tessa said. "What does it say?"

"It says 'I may be crazy, but at least I have each other.'"

16

Sherry struggled out of bed after another rough night. Her nightmares about the accident weren't diminishing at all. *Maybe I should talk to a counselor or something.* How did one go about finding a good counselor, anyway? If she could be sure she wasn't the driver, she often thought, she could get over the trauma of the accident and of having a good friend die. *Why can't I remember? I HAVE to remember!* Even in her dreams about the accident, she still had no recollection. It was beyond frustrating.

She stopped by the Bakery Café and got a cup of coffee and a cinnamon roll to take to her office. Setting them to one side on her desk, Sherry sat down and opened her computer. She was beginning to go over her list of rentals for the next few weeks when a tap at her door made her look up. Her boss, Steve, came in and sat in the extra chair.

"How are our rentals looking, Sherry?" he asked.

"Definitely down since Labor Day. Of course, I'm starting to get more for when the aspen turn and people come out for the colors."

He stood to leave. "Everything else going OK?"

"Sure. Fine."

"Look, Sherry, I know you're under a lot of stress from the accident and the court case coming up. If you need to take some time off, well, just say the word."

It took Sherry a moment to be able to get words past the lump in her throat. "Thanks, I appreciate that. For now, things are fine."

"OK. Well," he shrugged and headed out the door. "Keep me posted."

Sherry looked back at her computer and began scrolling through the rentals again. Of course, things were not fine. Her life was a roller coaster ride of feelings. One minute she'd feel like she had everything under control, then something would remind her of the accident and she'd feel as though the breath was knocked out of her. Just when she would think she had no more tears left, she would begin crying. The nights were terrible. She didn't know which was worse, lying awake worrying or falling asleep and having those nightmares. *I know I've got to get my emotions reined in, especially with a trial coming up. But, how?*

She sat back at her desk, put her hand on the computer's mouse and got back to work.

On Saturday, Sherry headed out in her car and turned up a secluded road. Sunflowers lined the way, their yellow faces reaching toward the sun, waving slightly in the gentle breeze. She drove to her favorite quiet place which overlooked the valley. This was her thinking place, and she had a lot of thinking to do. She put the window down, leaned back and breathed deeply. The air smelled clean and new with only a slight hint of the crispness of fall. The aspens whispered softly, while the ponderosa pines stood in silent majesty. It was only here that Sherry could feel the world begin to teeter back into alignment.

Then she let her thoughts go back to what was really happening in her life

How was she going to get over the nightmares and get a decent night's sleep? *Maybe I haven't fully faced the reality of the horror of the accident and the tragedy of Ed's death. I don't want to think about that because when I do, I always come back to the fact that maybe it was my fault. I can't bear to think about that!*

Sherry sat silently gazing at the peaceful view of the valley before her. She raised her eyes to the mountains, to the incredibly blue sky and puffs of clouds whose shadows on the mountains looked like some giant animal's paw prints bounding over the land. She was alone and the time was right. She got out of the car and walked a short distance to her favorite spot, a large outcropping of rock where she could sit. She had to face the demons inside her.

And so she did.

Roberta immediately noticed a change in Kay as she came down her steps Tuesday morning. There were smudges under her eyes indicating lack of sleep. Her mouth turned down, and her eyes were downcast.

Without even saying 'good morning,' she looked at Kay when she got in the car and said, "What's wrong?"

"That's the trouble with close friends," muttered Kay. "You can't even have a private life. They have to know everything."

"Well, so tell me. What's wrong?"

Kay sighed. "They called me yesterday. The hearing is set for October 14th. I'm to be prepared to be there and testify."

Roberta sat looking at her friend. She shook her head. "I don't know what to say that could possibly help. I do know that you'll get through this, and that we'll all be there for you. No matter what, though, this has to be so hard, Kay."

"It is. So awfully hard. I don't really want to talk about it at all. Let's go to breakfast."

"OK. At least we know Wanda will have some funny tee shirt to make us laugh."

When they got to breakfast, though, they were disappointed to find that Wanda had on a plain green tee.

"Wanda," Roberta wailed. "What's wrong? Why no profound statement on your tee shirt?"

"I couldn't decide if I was in a sassy mood, or a sarcastic mood, or what, so I went plain today. Sorry, girls."

"Speaking of moods," Annabelle began. "I was at the country club yesterday and saw Hannah Meyrick. She looked like she was close to a breakdown."

"What do you mean?"

"I spoke to her, and she almost jumped out of her skin. She was a nervous wreck. She tried to get herself under control. It was obvious that something was wrong. I asked her what was the matter. She said, 'It's a personal problem. I'll get it worked out soon'"

"I do feel sorry for her, trying to make everything work out for her daughter, and with her husband walking out on them."

"Did she say what kind of personal problem?" asked Myra.

"No, she didn't say anything else. My guess is that the challenges of trying to make enough money to live here plus put some aside for Shandra's college are simply becoming too much for her. Her daughter's college education has been her greatest priority ever since I've known her."

The group sat quietly, thinking of Hannah's plight.

"Did you feel that scent of autumn in the air today?" asked Roberta, steering the group to another subject. "I wonder when we'll have the first snow this year."

"It could be any time. We had it in mid-September a few years ago, remember?" remarked Wanda.

"It certainly is getting quiet around town," said Tessa. "Everyone is leaving. I had to say goodbye to Karen Pettersen on Sunday. I'll miss her wonderful smile."

Roberta nodded. "I don't know if it's because I'm getting older or what, but I've gotten to where I hate to say good-bye to people. I don't like any kind of change anymore."

Annabelle agreed. It was Olivia who spoke up. "In the first place, you all are not that old. In the second place, it's against our breakfast club rules to have such a somber, depressing breakfast. This is all your fault, Wanda, because you didn't wear one of your funny tee shirts."

Wanda held up her hands. "I'm sorry, girls. I'll do better next week."

The whole group smiled, and the conversations were light and airy for the rest of the breakfast, although Kay continued to remain quiet the entire time. Even with the end of somber talk each one carried a vague tendril of uneasiness with them when they left, though none could have explained why. It was as if when one heart held pain, the group heart carried that pain, and it slipped into each one's very core.

After the breakfast group broke up Myra did her errands, then checked her watch. It was 11:30. *That should be close enough to time for a lunch break.* She drove to the country club, parked and walked inside. She first checked out the lower floor. She didn't find what she was looking for and went upstairs. She looked up and down the hall and spotted Hannah vacuuming at the end by the lounge. She smiled to herself and strode down that way.

"Hannah," she said the name loudly to be heard over the noise of the vacuum cleaner. "Hannah," she said again, louder this time.

Hannah jumped and spun around. She shut off the machine. Putting her hand to her chest she said, "Oh, you startled me. Can I help you, Mrs. Stanhope?"

"Actually, I hope I can help you. Can you take a lunch break now? I'll buy you lunch at the grill. I want to talk to you about something."

A worried frown crossed Hannah's face. "Have I done something wrong?"

"I certainly hope not," Myra said. "No, I have a proposition for you. So, can you take your break now?"

"I guess so. They don't care exactly when I take it, just as long as I get the work done."

"Well, come on. Let's go have one of Earlene Durand's wonderful lunches."

"I have to put this away," Hannah gestured at the vacuum cleaner. "I'll meet you down there is a few minutes, OK?

Myra had settled herself at an outside table when Hannah joined her. They went inside to place their orders, and then returned to the table with their drinks.

Hannah was visibly nervous, Myra could see, so she began immediately. "I'm a person who gets right to the point of things."

Hannah nodded, her expression showing puzzlement and a little fear too.

"So, here's the thing," Myra said. "This is a small town and everyone knows everyone's business.

Hannah nodded again, looking more worried.

"It's no secret that your husband left you and Shandra, and that you're trying hard to stay here for her senior year and also prepare for the next year's college, am I right?

"Yes, but . . . " Hannah had drawn up straighter and now her expression became defensive.

Myra held up her hand. "Hear me out. I admire how hard you both are working. I also suspect that you can no longer afford the rent you were paying, yet you're unsure of where to go."

Tears began to pool in Hannah's eyes. She wiped them away, and they both sat still while the food was delivered.

"I happen to live in a big house that my husband left me with when he died. The basement level has two bedrooms, a bath, a living area and a small kitchen. It has its own entrance. I think it was originally meant to provide rental space for skiers and such. It's completely separate from my living space, and it's been empty for years since I don't want strangers coming in and out of my home. I would like to offer it to you and Shandra, rent free, for the duration of Shandra's senior year." She sat back and looked at Hannah, who sat stunned, with her mouth open and shock showing on her face.

"Well, what do you think?" asked Myra.

"I . . . I don't know what to think. You hardly know me. Why would you do that?"

Myra shrugged. "Why not?"

"I don't think I could accept such a generous gift. I . . . "

Myra placed her hand over Hannah's. "My dear young friend, I hardly think you're in a position not to accept it, are you? Where are you staying now?"

Hannah's lower lip trembled. She covered her face with her hands. "We've been living in our car since Sunday," she whispered.

"I thought so. That is not healthy for either of you. I know my idea sounds crazy, and I'm sure people in Angel Fire will think so. The truth is this will help both of us. You'll have a safe place for you and your daughter, a place that will not drain her college money, and I won't feel like a lonely, old lady rattling around in a big house by myself. It's a completely separate kind of apartment. We may not see each other often, if at all, even so, I'll know someone is there, and that will make me feel better."

Hannah took out a tissue and dried her eyes. "I don't know how I could ever thank you. How could I make it up to you?"

Myra smiled, patted Hannah's hand and pulled her own hand back. "When you get to be my age you know that doing for others brings the most joy back to yourself." She paused. "We need to eat up this good lunch." She took a big bite of her BLT sandwich and looked out toward the mountains.

17

"You look better this morning, Sherry," said her boss Steve, when she came in to work on Wednesday. "Are you finally sleeping well?"

Sherry nodded. "Yes, I'm doing better." She would never admit to anyone, even her daughter, the anguish she had gone through the past weekend as she had tried to come to grips with what was happening in her life. She went into her office and, while waiting for her computer to warm up, she allowed herself to think about the weekend.

After four hours at her thinking place, Sherry had walked back to her car. She felt completely spent. In the hidden solitude, she had allowed herself to grieve, to be angry, to face the tragedy of the accident. She finally had admitted to herself that Ed was someone who had been becoming more and more important to her, and that his death was a real loss. If the hearing proved that she was the driver, well, she would have to accept that and go on and continue to live her life as best she could.

She had sat silently in her car for a while that day, absorbing the peace of the valley scene before her, claiming some sense of that peace for herself. Finally, she had started the car and had driven home. That night, and for the next several nights, although the nightmares still came, they had somehow lessened in their intensity, and it was easier for Sherry to fall back to sleep.

Yes, I'm doing better, Sherry admitted to herself, *though I still have a long way to go. Would I do better if I remembered everything, or would that make things worse?* She had no idea.

After a full day at the real estate office, Sherry headed home. She made a salad for dinner, enjoying the everyday feeling of chopping tomatoes and carrots, mixing them with bits of Romaine, and topping them with her favorite balsamic vinegar dressing. After dinner, Sherry took her glass of Chardonnay out to the balcony and watched the light change from the almost magical clarity of pre-dusk that northern New Mexico is known for, to the time when the sun sinks behind the mountains in a last, golden glimmer. Artists come from all over the world to try and capture that unique light. Olivia told her once that it was impossible to paint it, that it was too ephemeral, that it was a kind of light that one wanted to reach out and touch, yet couldn't, even though it would seep into one's soul.

Sherry would never try to describe it, although she was always ready to experience it. Tonight she hoped for an Angel Fire sunset that looked like flames spreading across the sky. The sunset wasn't quite that, yet it was still beautiful. *I'm so sad that Ed was killed, but I'm still alive. I'm going to go on from this point and treasure the life I have.* Words of determination, which she hoped she could remember. She headed off to get ready for bed feeling that the weekend, followed by the routine of work that week, had done her a world of good.

Sherry woke with a start. She was shaking and damp from perspiration. Her heart raced and her breath came in gasps. Suddenly, she realized what she had been dreaming about. *The accident! I remember how it happened. Oh, my God, I remember! I remember it all now.*

She switched on the bedside lamp and grabbed the notebook and pen. The words were racing through her mind as she tried to write it all down.

We had gone to Walmart. I needed a new lipstick and some computer paper. Yes, I remember! Ed wanted—what? He wanted some shaving cream and something else. We walked out of Walmart. We went to the jeep and . . . and ED GOT IN THE DRIVER'S SEAT!

Yes, I remember! Ed was driving. We stopped at KFC for cokes, big ones. When we were just past the summit, a deer jumped into the road and Ed swerved. Oh, my God. I can see it all happening.

The cokes spilled in our laps and the ice was so cold. That's why we took off our seat belts. Yes! We were trying to swipe the ice cubes off our laps. It was crazy. Ed couldn't get the jeep right again. We were going all over the road, everything seemed to be flying around, and then—oh, God, I don't want to remember that part. It was like we were hurtling through the air.

Sherry felt the bile rise in her throat. She ran to the bathroom and was sick, over and over. She couldn't stop shaking. She sat on the bathroom floor, shivering and sobbing. "I wasn't driving. I wasn't driving," she whispered over and over. She sat huddled on the cold floor until the gray light of dawn eased through the window.

When full morning came and the rest of the world might be awake, and as soon as she thought he might be in his office, Sherry called her attorney.

"Phil," she began breathlessly. "You won't believe what's happened. I remembered. I finally remembered everything. All about the accident. Ed was driving, Phil. I could see it all plainly and I know he was driving."

She waited for Phil to exclaim about this revelation. There was no sound from the other end of the line.

"Phil, do you understand what I am telling you? I had a dream last night and I remembered everything."

"Yes, I understand, Sherry. The thing is, that's not really any kind of proof. I mean, it was a dream."

"Phil, don't you believe me? My memory came back. I remembered where we went and what we did. We got cokes from KFC. You can ask them. Maybe they remember seeing us and recall that Ed was driving."

"I believe you, Sherry. I simply don't want you to get your hopes up. What we need is a witness. Remember, they have a witness who says she saw you driving. Now it's her word against yours."

"Well, she is someone who had been dating Ed before. I didn't think she was the kind of person who would do that out of spite. Obviously she is because now I know Ed was driving. I'm certain of it, Phil."

"I know, Sherry. Sometimes our mind will play tricks on us, lets us believe things because we want to so desperately."

"But now I remember all the details leading up to the accident, every little detail."

"I hope that will be what we need."

"I'm going to call that state trooper who investigated the accident. He said to call if I remembered anything else."

"Good idea, Sherry. I'll work on things from this end. We have less than a month until the trial."

"Believe me, not a day goes by that I don't think about it."

After they finished their conversation, Sherry got out the paper Officer Thornton had given her and punched in the number. *I pray that he believes me,* Sherry thought as she drummed her fingers on the desk waiting for him to answer.

By Wednesday evening Hannah and her daughter were settled into the lower apartment of Myra's house. They both had tried to express their thanks to Myra. She brushed them off with a wave of her hand.

"I'm happy to do it," Myra replied. "And if you ever need a casserole for dinner some night, I keep a supply of them in the freezer in my garage. I've got chicken, rice, and broccoli, chicken fajita with rice and vegetables, chicken spaghetti with peas, and let me see, what else?" she paused to remember.

"Oh, that's all right," Hannah quickly said. "You've done more than enough for us, Mrs. Stanhope. We'll take care of our own food."

"And another thing. I think calling me Mrs. Stanhope is too formal. Besides, it makes me feel old. Please call me Myra."

"I'll try, Mrs . . . I mean, Myra."

The next Monday night Hannah knocked on the door separating the two areas when she heard Myra in the kitchen. When Myra opened the door, Hannah handed her a bunch of wildflowers; daisies, goldenrod, and asters. "Shandra picked these for you today," she said handing them to Myra.

"Why, how nice. They're so pretty. I'll put them in a vase."

"We want to let you know how much we appreciate what you're doing for us. There's no way we can thank you enough."

Myra smiled at her. "There's no need for that, Hannah. I told you that I'm glad to have you here. By the way, I've been meaning to tell you, there is that washer and dryer downstairs in the apartment and I'll have to get a plumber out to hook it up again. In the meantime, if you need one you can use mine up here."

"Well, if you really don't mind, I would like to do one load tonight."

"Go right ahead," Myra said, gesturing toward the laundry room.

After watching the local and national news and "Jeopardy," Myra walked into the kitchen to warm a can of soup and fix herself a sandwich. She turned to speak to Hannah in the laundry room next to the kitchen.

"Did you find everything you . . . " She stopped mid-sentence. Hannah was folding a blue towel with a bright yellow sun in the center that she had pulled from the dryer.

"What's wrong?" asked Hannah, a worried frown appearing on her face.

"Nothing," Myra started to say. "Actually, it's that towel. Someone mentioned to me that they saw that towel on the railing of the Smith's deck when the house was empty" She paused. "I'm guessing that the house wasn't empty, was it?"

Hannah's face paled, her expression full of horror. She put her hands to her face and backed away until she bumped into the wall. Sobbing, she slid down to the floor and rocked back and forth. "No," she wailed. "I never thought anyone would find out. Now, I'll have to go to jail! What will happen to Shandra? Oh, my God. What will we do? What will we do?"

"Now, hold on a minute," Myra said. "Settle down." She went to the microwave and took out the soup. "Let's go sit down in the living room and you tell me the whole story, the truth now."

Hannah continued to sit on the floor, sobbing uncontrollably.

Myra spoke more sharply. "Hannah, stop that. Come into the living room and tell me everything."

Hannah slowly got to her feet and wiped her face, which was blotchy from all her weeping. Myra pulled some tissues from the box on the counter, handed them to Hannah, and then took the box with her as she led the way to the living room.

When they were both seated on the couch, Myra said, "OK. Now begin at the beginning and tell me everything."

Hannah kept looking down. She could not meet Myra's gaze. "After Lance left us in the spring, we stayed at the apartment the rest of that month. I got the job at the country club right away, so they let us stay another month at the apartment. After that, I could see I'd never make enough money to cover all our expenses and still put some away for Shandra's college."

"Couldn't your family help?" asked Myra.

"It's only my parents, and they don't have two nickels to rub together. No, there wasn't anybody to help us."

"Did you go to the churches? I know they help people here in the valley."

"I did, but you can't keep going over and over. They'd helped us a lot in the past when Lance wouldn't work and was drinking so much." Hannah pulled two more tissues from the box and blew her nose.

"So what did you do next?"

Hannah took a deep breath. "I knew Sherry Sullivan took care of all those rental properties, so I asked her if I could have the job cleaning them. She knew what had happened to us, and she gave me the job." Hannah stopped and hung her head even lower.

"Go on," said Myra.

"Well, about that time, we had to leave the apartments. I stored most of our stuff at a neighbor's there, and then." She shook her head and held the tissues to her mouth.

"And then?"

"Shandra finished with school and got a couple of jobs babysitting and housesitting and all or would stay with friends, then she got the job at Zeb's. We started living in the car. That was hard. I'd see all these empty houses that I was cleaning, you know, and I thought . . . I thought well, why not? Who would ever know?" She looked up at Myra like a child pleading for understanding. "It wouldn't hurt anybody. We left each place exactly like we found it. If it was just me, I'd a gone back to Texas to my folks. But Shandra. I wanted so much more for her." Hannah's tears started again. "I'm sorry. I'm so sorry. I don't want to go to jail!"

Myra sat quietly, thinking through what Hannah was telling her, imagining what life was like for her. "Does Sherry know you were doing this?"

Hannah shook her head. "I don't think so. I started after her accident, and, of course, it was so much easier while she was gone. All the keys are in her office, and the master calendar is there, too."

Myra looked puzzled. "The Smith's don't rent their house out. Why were you staying there?"

"It was hard with the rental houses because we had to move around so much. The Smith's house was one Sherry's company was property manager for. They would check it once a week. We didn't eat there and hardly ever turned a light on or anything. All we did was go in at night and roll our sleeping bags out in a back hallway or something. We never touched their things or left a mess. We'd use the locker room at the country club for most of our showers."

Myra shook her head. "What a mess. What an unholy mess."

"I guess you want us to leave right away, huh? Are you going to turn me in?"

"You broke a law, you were trespassing, and you also broke the trust your employer had in you. That's a terrible example to set for your daughter." Myra shook her head again. "If I don't report you, I guess I'm aiding a criminal."

"Oh, Mrs. Stanhope, I'm so sorry! You were so kind to take us in, and now I've involved you in this horrible situation."

"That's true. We don't want to be hasty. We want to do the right thing for everyone. I think we should sleep on it tonight and tomorrow, when you get home from work, we'll talk about this again."

"You mean, we don't have to leave right now?"

Myra stood up. "You finish your laundry, and I'll have my supper. Try to get a good night's sleep and don't worry. I think there must be a way we can work this out." She gave a nod and a smile and went into the kitchen.

While she worked on making her sandwich she was aware of the sideways glances Hannah gave her as the laundry got folded.

It's going to be a long night, Myra thought.

18

The next morning, Hannah must have heard Myra come into the kitchen to get her car keys because she was tapping at the door that separated the two living areas. Myra opened the door and saw a poignantly haggard looking Hannah.

"Looks like you didn't sleep well," observed Myra.

"No, not at all. Well, what did you decide to do about me?"

"I haven't completely decided," Myra said. "There's a lot to consider. I don't want you stewing about it. I'll do what's best for everyone involved. I'm not going to throw you to the lions, Hannah."

Hannah's shoulders slumped. "What if throwing me to the lions IS the best thing?"

Myra looked at her watch. "I need to be going to meet friends for breakfast. We'll talk about this tonight when you get home. In the meantime, don't worry about it, don't even think about it. We'll get it worked out."

Hannah turned and walked down the stairs. It suddenly struck Myra how young and vulnerable her new guest looked. She sighed, shut the door, and headed out for the Bakery, where the JULIETs were having breakfast.

The Tuesday breakfast group was already gathering when Myra arrived. After placing their orders they sat around the big table catching up on news.

Myra waited until everyone was at the table. "I want to tell you all something." She looked around and it was obvious she had everyone's attention. "The other day when we were talking about Hannah Meyrick it sent up some red flags for me. I've been reading a lot about the plight of the working poor in our country, and about how many of them become homeless even though they're still working."

The group all nodded. The statistics were often told in thirty-second sound bites, although no solutions were ever offered.

"From Annabelle's comment, I couldn't help but wonder if Hannah and Shandra had found themselves in that position, perhaps were living in their car."

"Oh my," said Annabelle. "What a terrible thing that would be."

Myra looked her way, "Exactly what I thought. So, I went to her and we talked, and since that Sunday they had, in fact, been living in their car."

"How awful! We need to do something to help her," exclaimed Tessa.

"I wanted you all to know that I have invited them to live in that downstairs apartment at my house, and they accepted. They moved in last week."

"Myra, how good of you!" Roberta said.

"Not such a big thing," said Myra. "The apartment's been empty for years. It's just sitting there. Anyway, I'm glad there's someone else in the house, although we each have our own living area."

"Hannah is such a hard worker and so dedicated to her daughter. She deserves a break, if anyone does. Good for you, Myra." Olivia said.

"Yes, she does deserve a break," agreed Myra. *And that confirms my decision to keep her secret about the rental houses.*

"Myra, we'll rely on you to let us know if there's anything we can do."

"Sure will."

The conversations continued in the usual way, bits and pieces of their lives, knitting together. Wanda began laughing at something Olivia was telling her.

"Hey, no fair," said Roberta. "Our rules are that if you laugh about something you have to share it with all of us.

Wanda smiled. "You'll like this. You know how Sarah Kangerga gets so mad at the chipmunks that eat up her garden. Well, she traps them and sets them free behind one of the churches. Someone told her she must be hoping they'd get religion."

The friends laughed together, picturing Sarah giving the chipmunks a good talking to as she set them free.

That evening Myra knew that she could expect a knock on her dividing door as soon as Hannah got home from work, so it was no surprise when that knock came.

"Come and sit down," Myra said gesturing toward the kitchen table. "Do you want a cup of coffee or tea?"

Hannah shook her head. "No, thanks." She sat down on the edge of the chair, her hands gripped tightly together in her lap.

"I've given this situation a lot of thought," began Myra, sitting opposite Hannah. "There is no question about the fact that what you did was morally wrong and illegal. If Sherry had learned about it, she would have had no choice except to fire you and report you to the police. Even if she didn't want to, I'm sure her boss would have insisted on that course of action."

Hannah nodded. "I understand." She started to rise.

"Sit down, Hannah. I'm not finished."

Hannah sat, looking as if her world had ended.

"I've always believed in looking at the big picture, considering all aspects of a situation," Myra continued. "I see in you a dedicated mother, a survivor of difficult times. You didn't do what you did for any personal gain. You respected the places you went into. You have no need to continue to do what you were doing. So to my way of thinking, the best thing for me to do is to forget I ever learned about it."

Hannah's head came up sharply, and for the first time she looked at Myra. Her mouth opened in surprise. "What?"

"Turning you in would do no good for anyone. It might even jeopardize Sherry's job at a critical time for her. We will simply forget it ever happened."

Hannah sat with her hand to her mouth, tears pouring from her eyes. She was beyond words, her head shaking in disbelief at what she had heard.

"Now, there's no need to get all emotional about it," said Myra. "Life takes us down strange roads some times. We all simply need to do the best we can when we come to those twists and turns. I believe you tried to do that, even though what you did wasn't a good decision. As far as I can see, the road is clear now, clear for Shandra's senior year anyway." Myra stood up and pushed her chair back under the table.

Hannah stood and put her arms around Myra's solid body. Still, she had no words. In the evening light, in the small mountain community where Myra Stanhope believed that everyone's business was her business, Hannah Meyrick's sorrow and shame was replaced with the beauty of hope.

There are no words for that.

Another week went by, and with each passing day, Sherry became more and more worried. She had explained all she remembered to Officer Thornton, and he had come by her office once more to go over everything and to dutifully take notes. Sherry had no idea if he believed her or not.

"Did you question them at KFC? Did anyone remember seeing us?" she asked.

"I cannot really comment because this is an ongoing investigation," Officer Thornton said, slipping his pad in his pocket. He looked at Sherry, and for once his expression softened. "Off the record, though, I will say that, so far, no one could remember seeing you. After all, that was months ago and hundreds of people go past the drive through window, most they never even notice. I'm sorry." He stood to go.

"That's not fair! I know I wasn't driving, but how can I prove it?"

Office Thornton shrugged. "Remember, they're the ones that have to prove you were driving."

"And they have a witness," Sherry wailed. Suddenly, she had an idea. She would go to Kay and talk to her. Maybe she could make her see reason.

Day by day, as the case crept closer, the anticipation played a big part in the lives of a number of people. Sherry found it more and more difficult to concentrate at work. Her daughter had advised her against going to Kay directly, saying something about interfering with a witness might come out at the trial and actually hurt Sherry's case. With only ten days to go, the knot that developed in her stomach became more pronounced.

Kay was finding sleep harder to come by. She had gotten a prescription for a sleeping aid from the doctor. Even though she fell asleep, she woke up after a few hours and tossed and turned the rest of the night. She went over and over the memory of that day, and still the picture of Sherry and Ed walking out of Walmart, smiling and chatting, and then, of Sherry getting into the driver's seat was burned into her mind. She'd heard people in town saying that Sherry had regained her memory and remembered that Ed was driving. Kay wondered if she was losing HER mind. Did she really remember that Sherry was driving, or was that her own anger and hurt making her see things that really hadn't happened?

The Tuesday morning breakfast group was worried about Kay. As the trial approached, they could see Kay becoming more and more quiet, the bruise-like shadows under her eyes growing darker and darker. They tried keeping their breakfast conversation light and carefree. Wanda wore her funniest tee shirts. Olivia talked about how her nephew was working so hard to make up for his transgressions. Myra told how well Hannah and Shandra were doing, and shared several new casserole recipes she had made for them.

In spite of everything, though, the trial loomed closer and closer, and nothing could take away the strain.

As they finished up their Tuesday breakfast, Roberta said, "I'll be going to Taos tomorrow for the usual errands. Does anyone want to go?

Olivia held her hand up. "I need to go, thanks. Tell me what time and I'll meet you at Lowe's parking lot."

"Nine o'clock is good," replied Roberta.

Since the friends knew this would be the last breakfast before the hearing the next Tuesday, they had lingered over a second cup of coffee.

Finally Tessa said, "I've got to meet Jim for our hike today, so I'll say goodbye." She looked at Kay, but said nothing. The others also rose and, with the extra hug or squeeze of Kay's hand saying without words what friends say to each other, they bid their good-byes and left.

On the drive home, Roberta glanced at Kay. Although she was dressed attractively as always, Roberta noticed that Kay had lost weight. Her cheeks seemed to have sunk in giving her a gaunt look.

"You need to come with me to Taos tomorrow," Roberta said.

Kay looked at her. "Why? I don't need anything from Taos."

"That doesn't matter. You need to get out. All you'll do at home is worry more about the trial. Come on, it will do you good."

"No, thanks. I have to get the house cleaned. Heather will be here this weekend to spend the week with me."

"In the first place, your house is always clean," Roberta said with a smile. "In the second place, even if your house was a mess, you don't need to clean the house for your daughter."

Kay looked out the window for a moment. She sighed. "OK, I'll go."

"Good. Maybe we can have lunch at Yu Gardens or something. I'll pick you up at a few minutes before nine."

"Well, if Olivia is going, there's no point in being at Lowe's on time." A small ghost of a smile played on her lips.

On Wednesday, the three made their way over the pass and through the canyon to Taos. The cottonwoods along the creek had passed their peak golden color, and now the leaves made a golden brown carpet on the ground. Kay gazed out the window as they drove along.

"Fall used to be my favorite season. This year it makes me sad. It feels like the end of things, like death," she said.

"Oh, Kay, that sounds so sad." Olivia reached between the seats and patted Kay's shoulder.

Roberta frowned. "Well, the purpose of this trip, besides our errands, is to relax and enjoy ourselves, so let's talk about something pleasant."

Olivia immediately began telling them about a new place she had found that provided a beautiful setting for her paintings.

"I'd like to go there," Roberta commented. "It sounds beautiful."

"Better yet, buy one of my paintings of it and you'll always have it available without having to leave your house."

"Like everyone else in Angel Fire," Roberta retorted, "we have no wall space left after all the art auctions from Music and, now all the other organizations."

"Oh, well. I had to try," said Olivia. "So, what's our plan for the day?"

"Why don't we do Walmart first, browse Moby Dickens, and then have lunch? After lunch we can get our groceries."

Kay and Olivia approved the plan, and the three spent a relaxing morning together. After lunch they headed for Smith's, gathered their cloth shopping bags, and went their separate ways inside the store.

Roberta was getting her last items, some frozen vegetables, when Kay pushed her cart alongside.

"I'm done. How about you?" she said.

"This is the last," said Roberta. "What about Olivia?"

"She has a few more things. She said to go ahead and check out and she'll meet us at the car."

The two proceeded through the check-out line and loaded their things in the trunk of Roberta's car. They climbed in the front seat and sat back to wait for Olivia. A comfortable silence filled the car as the two friends leaned back, relaxed, and waited for Olivia.

Suddenly, Roberta said, "What?" and burst into laughter.

Kay sat up and looked around. "What's so funny?"

"I was looking for Olivia and I saw a young child climb in the driver's seat of that car parked behind us. It startled me for a minute, and then I realized what happened."

"What do you mean?"

"Well, the car is behind us, facing the same way we are, and I was looking in the mirror."

"So?" Kay's expression was puzzled.

'When you look in the mirror, things are reversed, so the child was really getting in the passenger side."

Kay's eyes widened, and the color drained from her face. With a gasp, her hand flew to her chest.

19

"Kay! What's the matter?" Roberta's voice was full of alarm. "Is it your heart?"

"I . . . I . . . That's how I saw them. That's how I saw Ed and Sherry! Oh, my God! I was in the Walmart parking lot and the jeep was parked a few rows behind me. I saw it after I parked and was looking in the mirror to see if I had any lipstick on before I went in the store."

"Behind you?" repeated Roberta.

Kay nodded vigorously. "Yes. I thought Ed must be there in Walmart, and I was looking forward to surprising him. I looked over my shoulder, and that's when I saw them"

"Ed and Sherry coming out of the store?"

"Right. So, I quickly turned back around and kind of slumped down so they wouldn't see me. I could still see them in the mirror. They were laughing and chatting together. I saw . . . that's when I saw Sherry get in the side that the driver is on. But she wasn't, was she? Oh, my God, Bertie. Do you realize what this means?"

Roberta nodded, her eyes shining with excitement. "Yes, this means that rather than testifying against Sherry, you can actually testify FOR her!"

Kay brought her hands to her face, a look of horror on her face. "What if we'd already had the trial? I would have destroyed her with a lie!"

"It wasn't a lie."

"It would have been if I'd testified. Oh, I've been so stupid, so terribly stupid!"

"Kay, stop. You were saying what you believed to be the truth."

"How stupid of me not to realize I was seeing the opposite. That never occurred to me, never."

"It's not too late to correct everything, Kay. As soon as Olivia gets here we'll go to the state police office and see if that investigating officer is there. We'll explain it all to him."

"How will I ever make it up to Sherry? She'll think I did it to be mean, out of anger."

Olivia opened the backseat door and started to put her grocery bags in. Sensing something was going on, she looked from Roberta to Kay and back again. "What happened?" she asked.

Words tumbling over each other, Roberta and Kay explained what they had discovered. "Oh, my gosh! That's amazing," said Olivia. She hurried with her bags, returned the cart, and jumped in the car.

Roberta turned onto the bypass and pulled into the parking lot of the state police headquarters. She had barely parked the car next to a state police car before Kay had the car door open and was hurrying out. "Come on," she called over her shoulder.

The three women entered the building, and were greeted by a state trooper. "What can I do for you?" he asked.

"Is Officer Thornton here?" Kay's voice was as breathless as if she'd been running up stairs.

"No. He's on a call up in the ski valley."

"When do you think he'll be back?"

"No telling, ma'am. Can I help?"

"I really need to talk to Officer Thornton. He's investigating a case I'm a witness for, and I realized I was all wrong. Things are the opposite of what I told him."

The officer looked at her with puzzlement on his face. "Excuse me?"

"Oh, it's too hard to explain. We'll wait if he might be coming soon. It's urgent that I talk to him." Frustration edged Kay's voice.

"I'll give him a call on his radio and tell him you're here. What's your name?"

"Mrs. Tucker. Kay Tucker."

"And what case is this about?"

"The accident up on the pass last June. It's supposed to go to court on Tuesday. But it can't now. That's why I need to talk to him. You see, I didn't realize about the mirrors."

"The mirrors?"

"I can explain the whole thing when he gets here. Please call and tell him I need to talk to him immediately."

"OK. Ma'am. Please wait right here."

It seemed like hours later to the three friends when Officer Thornton breezed through the office door. Kay shot out of her chair. "Thank heavens you're here," she exclaimed. "I need to change my testimony. It was actually the exact opposite of what I said, but I didn't realize it. Honestly, I didn't mean to tell it wrong."

Officer Thornton held up his hands. "Whoa," he said. "Let's go in my office and you can tell me from the beginning." He took off his hat and ushered Kay toward a back room.

Roberta and Olivia followed along.

"All of you?" he asked.

Kay gave him a quick glance. "Of course," she said.

Back in Angel Fire, Roberta had left Olivia off at the parking lot of Lowe's and then dropped a very excited Kay off at her home, before hurrying home to tell Al what had happened.

"That is amazing," Al remarked after Roberta shared the whole story. "What a quirk of fate that you noticed the child and made that comment."

"I know," agreed Roberta. "It gives me chills to think about it. It changes everything. Everything."

"And I guess now Kay is sure that's the way she saw Ed and Sherry that day, in the mirror?"

"Absolutely. If you're in a big parking lot where you don't have curbs or anything to correct your senses, and the cars are parked facing the same direction, it makes things look opposite from what they really are."

Al shook his head in wonderment. "Amazing," he said again.

As darkness blanketed around Kay's house she paced restlessly, her arms crossed against her chest. Had she done everything she needed to? She had told Officer Thornton everything, and he had written it all down. He said that he would contact both attorneys, and they would have to decide whether or not to go on with the hearing. She had asked him if she might call Sherry and explain everything to her. Although Officer Thornton discouraged her from doing that, he didn't say she couldn't. She had finally worked up her nerve and called Sherry to tell her. Sherry seemed so relieved that she had even thanked Kay for calling.

Kay wandered out onto the deck, feeling the ebony night wrap around her. She gazed up at the stars blanketing the sky. There was barely a breeze, just enough to feel like a gentle caress on her bare arms. The night was silent, resting.

Kay had called her daughter and told her the whole story, saying she didn't have to come up after all. However, Heather said they needed a visit and she had everything arranged so she'd be there on Monday, which greatly pleased Kay. What remained to be done?

"Ah, of course," Kay said aloud and smiled. She went into her room, switched on the light and picked up her Bible. She settled into her chair with a smile and opened the well-worn book.

Sherry hung up the phone after receiving the amazing message from Kay and collapsed into the nearest chair, laughing and hugging herself.

"I can't believe it! I really can't believe it." She said to no one there. She shook her head in wonder. *Oh, Ed, how could we have been so stupid as to undo our seat belts? This all would have been so different.*

She reached for her phone to call Amber. *But it wasn't different. It all really happened. So I'll have to live with what happened. And I'll have to go on with my life. That's all I can do.*

She punched the speed dial to reach her daughter.

The word had spread throughout the village before the Tuesday morning group met for breakfast again. As they gathered, the atmosphere was almost giddy. They were all smiling and exuberant in their greetings. Wanda's tee shirt said "We'll be friends until we're old and senile then we'll be new friends". Kay looked like her old self when she came in with her daughter.

After they were all seated, Roberta raised her coffee cup. "A toast. Here's to Kay for revealing the true story about the accident." They all raised their cups toward Kay. "Hear. Hear. To Kay," they said.

Kay was flushed and smiling. "It was such a fluke. We have Roberta to thank for mentioning about the mirror." They all raised their cups to Roberta and repeated the toasting.

"And here's to Sherry for all she's gone through, and for the burden that is no longer hanging over her." This time the group lifted their cups in silent tribute.

"And the amazing thing is," said Myra as they set their cups down, "that Sherry will get something from Ed's insurance. What a great turnaround of events."

"Speaking of the accident reminds me," said Myra. "You all know Sammy, the tow truck driver? I'm sure he would have been the one who pulled the jeep back up. Well, I heard he's been arrested for selling drugs."

"Really?" said Annabelle. "I thought he was such a nice young man when he pulled our car out of the ditch that time."

"Well, he's evidently not so nice. He had quite a business selling prescription drugs, especially oxycodone."

"How did they catch him?" asked Olivia.

"It was pretty stupid of him. He had spilled a huge bottle of pills in his tow truck. I guess he thought he'd picked them all up, but there were still a few on the floor. When he was pulling some car out of a ditch with the police there, his truck door was opened and the policeman saw the pills. Pretty careless."

Tessa sat back and pictured the pills she had found at the accident site. *So, that explains it.* She smiled and sipped her coffee.

Roberta looked around the group of friends as several different conversations were going on at one time. *I love Tuesday mornings,* she thought with a satisfied smile. *And I'm so thankful for these women, these special friends. One never knows how life will unfold, what twists and turns the road will take . Isn't it wonderful when we can share the ups and the downs and, most of all, the joys in our lives?*

Annabelle quietly set her coffee cup down. For days she had been mulling over the information she had heard about whether or not Sherry or Ed had been in the drivers' seat at the time of the accident. In her precise mind, she knew that it was possible under certain circumstances for things to seem reversed in the mirror. Evidently, that had been enough for Ed's family and the lawyers to decide not to pursue the case. She also knew that the premise for the reversal of positions in the mirror was not factual. It was a spatial concept in which probably only left brained people saw the difference. Images would be reversed (such as letters) but positions would not be reversed when seen in a mirror, thus a person entering on the passenger side would always be seen on the passenger's side and not the driver's side.

Did this mean that Ed actually had been the driver, or not? wondered Annabelle. She shrugged, and simply let it go.

Maybe . . . but maybe not.

MYRA'S FAVORITE CASSEROLES

Chicken Dinner in a Dish (Ethel Sorrells)
(contributed by Dean Calhoun)

1 chicken, boiled and chopped
½ cup celery, chopped
4 hardboiled eggs, sliced lengthwise
¼ cup melted butter
¼ cup plain flour
½ teaspoon salt
¼ teaspoon pepper
1 cup milk
1 cup chicken broth
1 small onion, thinly sliced
¼ cup chopped green pepper or pimento strips

Place celery, chicken and eggs in casserole dish (9x13).

Blend butter, flour, salt and pepper. Gradually stir in broth and milk. Bring to a boil. Add onion and green pepper. Pour over chicken mixture. Bake in 425 degree oven while making cheese biscuits (about 10 minutes).

Cheese Biscuits
2 cups sifted (self-rising) flour
¼ pound cheddar cheese, grated
1/3 cup cooking oil
2/3 cup buttermilk

Stir grated cheese into flour. Add oil and milk, all at once. Stir with a fork until mixture forms a ball. Knead 10 times to make a smooth dough. Take a small portion of dough at a time; roll thin; cut biscuits to place on chicken. There will be left over dough. Continue baking

Character Builders Spaghetti
(contributed by Sylvia Hornback)

4 chicken breasts, cooked and deboned
1 can mushroom soup
1 can chicken soup
1 pound thin spaghetti
1 cup whole or skim milk
1 pound Velveeta cheese (melted)
1 stick butter
1 chopped green pepper
1 large onion, chopped
1 can Rotel tomatoes

Boil chicken, sauté onions and green pepper in butter, add soups and Rotel tomatoes, next add Velveeta cheese and milk, then add cut up chicken.

Cook spaghetti in chicken broth (cut spaghetti into shorter lengths, this makes it easier to mix together.)

Mix all together. Put in a 9 X 13 baking dish and cover lightly with grated cheddar cheese. (Can be frozen at this point.)

Bake at 325 degrees until thoroughly heated (about 30 minutes if at room temp. It will take longer if it is frozen.)casserole for 20-25 minutes. Cut and bake remaining biscuits for 12-15 minutes.

Buttermilk Mashed Potatoes
(contributed by Carolin Sanders)

4. Lbs. baking potatoes, peeled and cut into 2-inch pieces
3. Tsp.salt, divided
¾ cup warm buttermilk
½ cup warm milk
¼ cup butter, melted
½ tsp. freshly ground black pepper

1. Bring potatoes, 2tsp. salt, and water to cover to a boil in a large Dutch oven over medium-high heat; boil 20 minutes or until tender. Drain well. Reduce heat to low. Return potatoes to Dutch oven, and cook stirring occasionally, 3-5 minutes or until potatoes are dry.

2. Mash potatoes with a potato masher to desired consistency. Stir in buttermilk, milk, butter, black pepper, and remaining 1tsp salt, stirring just until blended. Spoon the mixture into a lightly buttered 21/2 qt. baking dish or 8 (10 oz.) ramekins.

3. Bake at 350* for 35 minutes. Serve warm.

***To make it "Angel Fire worthy" stir in ½ cup chopped green chilies, 11/4 cups pepper jack cheese and ½ cup finely chopped cooked chorizo sausage prior to baking.

REUBEN CASSEROLE
(contributed by Susan Stuart)

8 ounces wide noodles, cooked
3 Tablespoons butter
1 pound sauerkraut, drained
2 cups chopped corned beef
2 medium tomatoes, peeled and sliced
¼ cup Thousand Island Dressing
8 ounces shredded Swiss cheese (2 cups)
4 crisp rye crackers, crushed
½ teaspoon caraway seed

In a greased 9x13 pan layer buttered noodles, sauerkraut, corned beef and tomatoes. Dot with salad dressing and sprinkle with cheese. Top with cracker crumbs and caraway seed.

Bake covered at 350 degrees for 40 minutes. Uncover and bake about 15 more minutes or until bubbly.

CHIPMUNK AND KALE CASSEROLE

(contributed by Sarah Kangerga)

4 medium potatoes
4 Tablespoons butter
2 Tablespoons oil
½ lb small white onions, peeled
6-8 chipmunks, cleaned
Salt & pepper
½ cup dry white wine
½ cup bourbon
2 teaspoons instant beef boullion
½ lb fresh mushrooms, sliced
1 ½ lb fresh kale

Cut potatoes lengthwise into 4 sections. Melt butter and oil in flame-proof skillet or casserole over direct heat. Add potatoes and onions and saute until golden. Remove vegetables and set aside. Brown chipmunks. Sprinkle with salt and pepper. Add wine and bourbon and ignite. When flames subside, add boullion and blend well. Add mushrooms, kale, onions, and potatoes. Cover tightly and bake at 350 degrees for 1 hour, or until tender (if that ever happens), basting occasionally.

CHEESY CHICKEN AND RICE CASSEROLE
(contributed by Becky Jones)

Serves 6 – 8

1 cup uncooked long grain rice

2 cups fresh or frozen vegetables (sautéed in oil and garlic) Becky suggests broccoli, carrots and red pepper

1 can cream of chicken soup

1 1/3 cups water or 1 can chicken broth

1 cup sour cream

4 skinless, boneless chicken breasts, cooked and seasoned with salt, pepper and herbs

1 cup pepper jack cheese, grated

1 – 2 cans chopped green chilies (to taste)

Stir together soup and water or broth and sour cream (Becky prefers broth and sour cream), rice, some cheese, seasonings and vegetables in a 12 x 8 casserole dish. Top with chicken and some cheese. Bake at 375 degrees for 45 minutes or until chicken is done. Top with remainder of cheese.

Be sure to use one small breast per person or cut larger breast in half.

Double recipe makes two 9 x 13 casseroles and generously serves 8 each and is great for a buffet.

Can also slit breasts and stuff with seasonings or cheese.